The Autobiography of Satan

(Authorized Edition)

William A. Glasser

Published by Open Books

Cover image "DORÉ, Gustave Illustration for John Milton's Paradise Lost 1866" via carulmare at www.flickr.com/photos/8545333@N07/

ISBN-10: 099842742X / ISBN-13: 978-0998427423

1

Do you want to be one of this world's damn fools, swallowing everything spoon-fed to you, or do you want to start thinking for yourself?

Why, you ask, with your usual suspicions, should you pay attention to anything I say? It's a reasonable question. Why, indeed? Your distorted sense of me has persisted for much too long now, and to your own detriment, I might add, for it has been used incessantly to scare you into an unquestioning state of submission. There have been far too many twisted accounts of me, both mythic and legendary—and all, of course, unauthorized. Deep inside the mental pockets of your memory, generally out of sight and mind, you carry around these delusional tales like small, polished, talismanic stones that have the power, if the need ever arises, to ward off any approach I might make toward you. But all they have accomplished thus far is to keep you unaware of what is lurking beneath them, the insidious web of secrets that, across the ages, has so cleverly been kept hidden from you. My aim, as you will see now, if you can only look with open eyes, is to awaken you to the truth of my existence. Believe me when I say that my deepest desire has always been to tell you the truth, and nothing but the truth, so help me—even though, for thousands of years, I have been branded the Father of Lies. Talk about a bum rap.

Picture a hairy, red-faced character, with horns, claws, and a pointed tail, a sulphur-smelling, demonic figure, wearing a hideous grin as he pitchforks soul after salacious soul into the burning depths of Hell. Can you imagine any reasonable individual swallowing such a silly explanation for why evil exists in this world?

But I am obviously getting ahead of myself. This is, after all, the story of my life.

*****

Did you get all of that down, Wag, or do I have to repeat it?

I got it. I got it. What can I say?

Do not say anything. Just keep writing. That scritchy-scratchy sound of your quill, it helps me think. Gives me ideas. Calls up old memories I need to bring back now.

Is that why you won't get me a laptop?

Oh, no. Not that again.

Why not?

Just keep writing.

2

Considering the raging flames of Hell, so often viewed as swirling around me, I find it rather ironic that I first came into existence during an unusually cool evening in the midst of an ancient African jungle. The most advanced life-forms to be found there at that time were some barely human, shaggy creatures who were still struggling to stand erect in a world that was all but daring them to survive. The event took place in a small clearing, beside a brook that was meandering through it. One of the creatures was squatting there, resting for a moment after drinking from the brook. Aimlessly looking around, he happened to glance down at a rock lying near him. The rock was darker than the others that were scattered along the edge of the brook. Lifting one of the others, he hefted its weight and stared at it for a moment. Then he raised it above his head and brought it down sharply on the dark rock, wanting to see it break into pieces, as others had done before whenever he struck them. But this time, in the dim evening, as the rocks made contact, a bright spark flew out toward him, startling the man and causing him to sit back onto the ground.

And, at that moment, like the tiny spark, I flickered into existence.

With his heavily-browed, deep-set eyes opened now in wonder and fear, he watched the rock closely, waiting to see what else it might do.

Looking back, I can recognize, of course, that it was not a very propitious beginning, for that shaggy creature's fearful response would prove to be the very first step toward what unfortunately lay ahead for me.

My misplaced, undeserved, accursed reputation.

The one, by the way, that you are still carrying around.

Before we move ahead, however, down the darkened hallways of prehistory, you might want to pause here, for just a moment, and think of what you have already revealed to me about yourself by opening the pages of my life.

*****

Who are you talking to? Who is you?

A good question, Wag. Right to the point. It involves a basic authorial decision regarding the—

Forget I asked.

Why, Wag? I like your question.

Then why don't you answer it? In just a few words.

Because I have in mind, Wag, someone whose nature is a bit more complicated than that.

I think it's because you never answer any

question in just a few words.

Is that really true?

Don't you think I know? Scratching out each of your words? A laptop, you know, can count the number of words you use.

Quill time again, Wag.

3

*W*e step ahead now to another revealing moment that will require a more focused effort from you if you are going to share the experience at all, for I doubt if you can even recall the last time you actually faced the unknown. And I do not mean something that you simply did not know. I mean a presence that you felt was lurking somewhere just beyond the edges of your awareness, a presence that filled you with a sense of dread.

It did not take long, within that early world, before a scattering of other individuals began, not only to sense my existence, but to grope about for some way to bring themselves into my presence. Why, you may well ask, considering the fear I had already aroused, would anyone want to do such a foolish thing? The answer awaits us in the midst of that unfolding moment.

It is evening now, and rather chilly outside, so let us go in and join that small group of paleolithic men.

They have gathered, along with their women and children, around the fire blazing just inside that wide entrance to the large cave. The men have come together to seek me out, for they want something from me. They will be led on their quest by the sorcerer of the group, who believes he knows exactly where he can find me and how to bring me forth.

After they shuffle around together in the warmth of the fire, the sorcerer raises his voice, and the men begin to separate from the women and children. At the rear of the cave is a small opening leading into an intricate branching of passageways running far back into the earth. They are about to make their way to a place that only the men are allowed to enter, a small chamber hidden in the very deepest part of the cave.

Each of the men lights a torch at the fire and carries a second, unlit one. The women and children are hushed now, for the time has come. As the men move away from the fire, they fall in behind the sorcerer, and then disappear, one by one, into the small opening at the rear of the chamber. The entry to the narrow passage brightens for a moment as they pass into it with their torches, silhouetting each of their short, heavy bodies, before the darkness closes in behind them.

What lies ahead within the depths of that darkness they are entering? Let us fall in line with them, and see for ourselves.

Except for the sounds of their shuffling feet, the men advance in silence, single-file, their torches held above them. In the crystalline limestone walls of the cave, the flickering reflections from the light are like the blinking eyes of a thousand animals.

Moving deeper into the earth, they begin to feel a presence now as the darkness seems to thicken around them. There is something ahead, something unknown, waiting for them. Finally, after a seemingly endless walk, they reach the last passage, which spirals steeply upwards, as though it is challenging them to enter. They make the climb with muted, guttural sounds of exertion, and then stumble from the passage, one by one, into the small chamber at the top. With widened eyes and heavy breathing, they press against each other in the small space, seeking for some added protection in the group.

Gripping their torches more tightly now, they are quickly silenced by what they see. On a raised ledge to one side within the chamber, a figure slowly looms up before the group and stands there looking down upon them. A few of the members murmur uncomfortably as they see the change in their sorcerer. On his hands are the paws of a cave-bear, and he is wearing the ears of a timber wolf now. He stares at them, motionless, until he has their complete attention. Then he begins to move back and forth along the ledge, imitating the motions of different animals, the cave-bear suddenly rising up, the timber wolf crouching before it attacks, as he gropes to enter a world much deeper than the one they walk upon. The members of the group silently watch him, fascinated now, as he attempts to call forth, and bring up before them, their sadly distorted image of me. The sinister source of all their troubles.

Their hunting excursions, for much too long, have not fared well, and the group's food supply is now dangerously low. At critical moments, during their hunts, something bad always happens. A bird nearby flutters up, and the approaching animal veers from its path. Or the spear that does strike an animal is not enough to bring it down, and the wounded beast, with a warning roar, flees with the others out of range. Having faced so much bad fortune, they are now seeking out its source within the deepest region of the cave. When the morning comes, they will leave the cave to hunt for the swift and elusive red deer that have been spotted recently in their area. They have gathered here now to ask me not to place any further obstacles in their way.

The sorcerer slowly and solemnly moves to one side of the ledge. He bends down over a small basin carved in the rock. Dipping his now bared hand into the basin, he brings it forth covered with a red liquid and turns to face the wall at the rear of the ledge. With deft movements of his hand, and repeated dippings in the basin, he paints upon the wall, to the amazement and delight of the group, the figure of a red deer. There it stands before them now, the animal they will soon hunt. They nudge each other as the excitement grows. In the morning, the red deer will surely appear before them now.

Plunging his hand once more into the liquid, the sorcerer turns again to the wall. He begins to paint a smaller spot now. It puzzles them. What is he doing? They can make out nothing, as they watch from below, but a red blur behind his hand. With a few quick motions, however, he begins to transform the blur for them into the shape of an emerging face. Like the wavering light from their lifted torches, their tension is almost visible now. The moment they have been waiting for, hoping for, is about to arrive.

Turning away from the wall now, the sorcerer leaves the red face hanging there above them, like a painted mask, but with nothing behind it. Sensing their growing anxiety that he will not be able to call me forth, he slowly turns back to the wall, and, with a few more carefully placed touches, the sorcerer now awakens the face for them. As though the mask had suddenly come to life, its eyes, more deeply reddened now, seem to be glaring angrily down at the group.

The sorcerer then drops to his knees on the ledge. When he lifts his arms up toward the wall, like a supplicant imploring the face upon it, the members below are stunned to silence. They all stare up now in trembling awe, for they are convinced that the sorcerer has finally brought me forth for all of them to see.

And for me, regretfully, to see all of them, as they mimic their sorcerer and fall in fear, one by one, onto their knees.

4

There were indeed a good many intimidating moments that held those early people in thrall. And there were also, as you might well assume, disruptive times of intense fear, when their minds were caught and twisted by unexpected terrors. As they continued opening their wary eyes to the bewildering world that was moving around them, it did not take them long before they were seeing a multitude of harmful forces popping out all over the place, like hemlock weeds and deadly nightshade. When they discovered that they were completely at the mercy of those forces, and that their very survival was often at stake, they struggled desperately to understand the workings of their world. The harmful forces were clearly evil. They began to give names to them.

I am counting on you, as we move ahead here, to keep your eyes open as you take in their world, for I want you to experience, once again, what it felt like to exist at that early time.

Every day that you are awakened by the morning light, you sense the presence of those unpredictable forces around you. You are at their mercy, and anything can happen. Today, in the midst of a thunderous storm, lightning strikes a nearby tree in the forest, setting off a fire, and the flames, fanned by a gusty wind, spread quickly and rage through the forest, and then out across the plains, until they have almost encircled you. Following the frantic members of your group, you flee in terror to a small lake close at hand, where you splash into the water and squat down to avoid the heat of the approaching flames. Then you cower there, your mind gripped by fear, as you watch what is taking place around you. As far as you can see in all directions, the animals and the plants that live around the lake, including the very ones you depend on for food, are destroyed or disappear from sight as the devouring fire sweeps in and consumes your world.

The night comes early, darkening the land, and you stay in the water, shivering from the cold. Throughout the night you watch the flames flickering among the shadows that are slowly creeping back now into the forest. When the morning comes, the fire dies out, and breezes begin to clear away the smoke. Leaving the lake, chilled to the bone, you return with your group to the land and face what awaits you there. You walk on warm ashes now. Carefully, you make your way between still smoldering trees burnt down to charred trunks. In the sky above, dimmed by the lingering smoke, the morning sun is pale and feeble. The anguished eyes of those around you reflect back your own painful feelings. The world you have known for so many years has been taken from you.

Who could have done such a terrible thing? Who had rumbled and tumbled the clouds and lashed the trees with those wild winds? And who had flashed down that frightful lightning? You look up above you now, with a mingling of fear and anger, and you sense, somewhere in the sky, the presence of a storm-god. Only a powerful and destructive god, an epitome of *evil*, could wreak such havoc upon the earth. But who was this storm-god? What was his name? Down through the many ages of human existence, I have been infested with a seemingly endless swarm of names and titles. Belial. Azazel. Baal. Dagon. Moloch. Astaroth. Asmodeus. Tchort. Puki. Ahriman. Typhon. Apophis. Semiramis. Leviathan. Lucifer. Beelzebub. Mephistopheles.

On and on, without end.

The Serpent. The Dragon. The Tempter. The Adversary. The prince of darkness. The god of this world.

Generally, I am not bothered by such mean and petty name-calling. Sticks and stones. You know what I mean. And yet that last one, the god of this world, now that one, out of all the others, really hurt.

You, of course, at this point, cannot yet imagine why.

Or can you?

What a pleasant surprise that would be.

5

After those early people began giving names to the unseen forces, only a small bit of effort was needed to take the next obvious step: picturing them in the mind's eye. Fearsome figures of all sizes and shapes began to arise now into the light of day out of the darkness lurking beneath human thought. They were often pictured as having human forms, but with a variety of beastly parts stuck on, the horned head of a bull, an eagle's claws, a lion's haunches, what have you.

Yes, of course, their imaginations were running wild. It was the only tool they had for shaping their world into something that made sense to them. And yet, apparently, you just mentally shrug, for you find no surprise in the way they acted. Those mythic images, after all, were just something out of a distant age, something that faded away long ago with the passing of those early people. But, if that is the case, then how would you explain the horns and the tail you keep sticking onto me?

If you are going to picture a figure of evil, you might begin by at least giving a moment's thoughts to the nature of evil. As you might expect, evil is a subject that intensely interests me. It is one with which I am deeply familiar, and I will be visiting it frequently from this point on. And so will you, if you tag along, for I have woven into the fabric of my life an enlightening pattern that you should see. I want to open your eyes to the true source of evil in this world.

Yes, I can imagine you glancing my way once again. But are you really convinced that you have the answer? Without any doubt? Any at all? Perhaps you had better pause here again. Look back over your shoulder now.

Can you remember who first fed you that answer?

*****

Did you see the point I was making here, Wag?

No, I don't have time for that. It's all I can do to keep up with you. You're not a slow talker, you know.

Yes, I see. And the quill and ink. That must, at times, make it even harder.

What do you mean, at times? It's always hard. Scratching out each word by hand. Did you know that a laptop printer can turn out eight pages a minute?

No, Wag, I did not know that. My thoughts, at the moment, are in the past.

Already dead, you mean? Inside your head? That can really mess you up.

Not dead, I hope, Wag. Some thoughts can live for a very long time.

And some of them are like fish, aren't they? Belly-up before you know it. And then what happens? After just three days? So strong, it'll knock you down.

What are you telling me now, Wag? That, in three days, these thoughts you are writing down will reek like a dead fish?

No, you don't have to wait that long. Why do you think I keep turning the page?

6

$\mathcal{A}$ few more quick steps through history now. Why a few? And why quick? Because I am all too aware of the pathetically short attention spans that are out there among so many easily distracted people. I have seen ants pulling a bit of something through the grass give more attention to what they were doing. If I were in the midst of telling them the secrets of this universe, revealing to them all that lies beyond the edges of human awareness, they would probably be yawning by now and looking around for something more diverting. There is only one way to hold their weak and wavering attention. Just offer them, from the bottom of the barrel, the dregs of anything entertaining.

Well, they should not hold their breath. I am not here to entertain them. I have something much more insidious in mind for them.

Let me open this small window for you, and we will watch that group of Stone Age women, the particular ones over there, for they have been out searching all day for the wild plants that are eaten by their larger group. Finding a few here, and a few there, they had slowly gathered them into armloads that they each brought back to their living place and dumped onto the ground into a common pile to be shared by the small children left behind and by the men who had gone off hunting.

As that particular pile was consumed over a number of days, what remained on the ground were a few scattered seeds that, watered by a brief rain, had begun to grow. They could easily have been ignored and trampled underfoot in the daily activities of the group. But I nudged one of the women back over to that nearby spot on the ground, where she bent down and stared at the germinating seeds. She remembered the long and tiring day they had all spent in searching for the sparsely scattered plants. And yet here they were, growing before her. Her eyes widened with a new awareness.

Yes, you heard me correctly. I was the one who urged them. And they certainly needed my help here, for it was something entirely new to them. Since there was no supermarket in sight yet, they were left with only two choices. They could continue going out each day and tediously gathering the food they needed, if, indeed, it was there at all. Or they could try, with their new awareness, to cultivate the wild plants and the dead animals they kept bringing back in scrabbled handfuls and occasional armloads.

Their attempts were rather tentative and stumbling at first, but, by trial and error, these new approaches, to my great delight, began to flourish.

Unfortunately, however, as these exciting activities

continued arising in their midst, the planting and harvesting, the birthing and herding, some old, entrenched mind-sets also erupted forth. Like mushrooms testing the light of day, new rituals of worship arose, attuned now to the seasonal cycles of growth and death, and they spread like wildfire throughout their world.

The Akkadians had the sun-god Belus conquering the winged beast Tiamat. The Babylonians and the Assyrians had their hero Gilgamesh battling with the monster Huwawa. The Mesopotamians had the war-god Ninurta defeating the water-demon Azag. The Egyptians had Osiris battling with Set, the demon of evil and death. The Greeks had Zeus battling with Typhon, the offspring of Tartarus who was suckled by the Delphian Dragoness. On and on, with no apparent end, heroes and gods continued arising and doing battle with a host of evil forces threatening to disrupt the workings of the natural world. And as they each emerged, as might be expected, an ominous question also arose.

Who, among them all, deserved to be worshiped? Who was the true god?

Step forward now and hold out your hand. I would like to introduce you to the prophet Zoroaster, who entered the scene in ancient Persia back in the sixth century BC. (And, yes, you can stop that muted snickering. I know what BC means.) When Zoroaster looked at the world around him with his two brooding eyes, he found his own deepest beliefs being reflected back to him. One eye saw a supreme god who represented the light, everything truthful, and all that was good. The god was named Ahura Mazda, the Omniscient One. He was depicted as a bearded man with a winged body. It struck me at the time that wings by themselves were at least an improvement, somewhat more appealing than a lion's haunches. Zoroaster's other eye saw Ahriman, a fiendish figure of darkness and evil. His symbol was the serpent. Yes, the serpent. Not the one you know, of course. But have a bit of patience, for yours will slither into sight very shortly now.

And so, in the fiery furnace of Zoroaster's mind, the hammer blows of his own beliefs shaped good and evil into two deified figures, each with a distinctive role to play. Ahura Mazda had brought forth a perfect world, created with order, and infused with a law that revealed his presence. A rather nice idea, if you think about it. Something like a cosmic Garden of Eden. However, Ahriman then intruded in the creation, disrupting the order, and entering into what would become an eternal war.

Yes, I know. It sounds somewhat familiar. A different cast, but the same play.

When Zoroaster made his way east to the kingdom of Bactria, he managed to arouse, in the Bactrian king, another inevitable response to his teachings. The king was also a warrior, and since he now believed in Zoroaster's vision, he was willing to do battle against any other belief, convinced that Zoroaster's god, the Omniscient One, would lead him to victory. Throughout the lands, it became a game of one-upmanship among the many different believers. "My god is better than yours. My god is stronger than yours, more victorious in battle, omnipotent, omniscient, omni—what have you. And your god does not deserve to be worshiped. Your god is a false idol." They took it as far as their thoughts would let them. "My god created everyone and everything that exists, both heaven and hell, and all between, and whatever else might come to mind."

Do you see any problem here? Any at all?

*****

Don't tell me. Another one?

Another what, Wag?

Another question, without any answer.

Those are the kind I like best.

You're fooling me now. Is that right? What you said, it doesn't make sense.

No, I am not fooling you. Just take a moment. Think about it. What do you do if you have no answer?

I don't know. I guess I shrug. And then I ask you. What's the answer?

But why turn to me, Wag?

Because I already said I don't know. And you're the one with all the answers.

No, Wag. You have that wrong. I am the one with all the questions.

What does that mean? Anybody can ask questions. Sounds like a cop out to me.

It means, Wag, that, to find an answer, you have to keep asking more questions.

Have you ever been on a merry-go-round? I bet you have. Sounds like it.

A merry-go-round? Why do you ask?

Round and around. And where does it get you? Right back to where you started.

I see what you mean, Wag. Round and around. It takes me right to my next question.

Something, I bet, about turning the page. Maybe it's time, on that merry-go-round, to get yourself a different horse. And a shovel, too.

Why a shovel?

Pick up what that horse keeps dropping, before people are stepping in it.

Are you talking about my story, Wag?

Another question, without an answer.

7

The problem, of course, is the origin of evil.

You, apparently. without any doubt, remain convinced that you already know, for you are still faithfully carrying around someone else's answer. And it seems that you are not in the least confused by that answer, even though, across the ages, it has addled so many inquisitive minds. So help me out here. I would like to understand. I really would.

Try to envision, if you can, a loving and benevolent god, one who is also omniscient and all-powerful. Has your god created everything in the universe? If so, then who created evil? Not your benevolent god, you say. Everything he does is good. Then what is the source of evil? Another god? An evil god? But who created that god? If your god did, then he still created evil. And if he did not, then the evil god has a separate existence. And since he is able to bring evil into your world, your god must be less than all-powerful.

Can you reason your way out of this dilemma? Give it a try. See where it leads you. Your benevolent god did create the other god, but he made him good, as he does all things. Then the other god did things on his own that turned him evil. That would certainly explain it.

But you said that your god was omniscient as well as omnipotent. If so, then at the moment he created the other god, he must have known that his act would bring evil into the world.

Yes, but he still allowed it to happen, for he wanted to use that evil god to inflict punishment upon the sinners of this world.

What is that, you say? The sinners of this world? Where did they come from?

Well, originally....

How many angels can sit on the point of a pin?

It boggles my mind when I think about the inexhaustible mental efforts that have been expended across the ages to explain away the nature and the source of evil. Most of those efforts have been repetitious and rather awkward attempts to keep piling all evil, in whatever form it appeared, squarely upon my shoulders. Do you have even a glimmering by now of what is indicated by that monstrous mistake? My reputation, so far off the mark, and so blatantly undeserved by this point, continued to go to hell, so to speak. As you will see.

Let us stroll here for a moment in the cool of day through one of the world's best known tales. The Garden of Eden. We pick it up in the middle.

Now the serpent was more subtil than any beast of the field which the LORD God made. And he said unto the woman, Yea, hath God said, Ye shall not eat of every tree of the garden? And the woman said unto the serpent, We may eat of the fruit of the trees of the garden: But of the fruit of the tree which is in the midst of the garden, God hath said, Ye shall not eat of it, neither shall ye touch it, lest ye die. And the serpent said unto the woman, Ye shall not surely die: your eyes shall be opened, and ye shall be as gods, knowing good and evil.

And so Eve eats the fruit, and gives some to Adam, who also eats. Then God comes down and appears in the garden, and when he sees that Adam is afraid, because he now knows he is naked, God says,

Hast thou eaten of the tree, whereof I commanded thee that thou shouldest not eat?

You should begin to get somewhat suspicious here. It is beginning to look like a set-up. A sting operation. This God, after all, is supposed to be omniscient. He must have known they would eat the fruit when he created them. Adam, by this point, should be crying "Entrapment!" But what does he do, instead?

And the man said, The woman whom thou gavest to be with me, she gave me of the tree, and I did eat. And the LORD God said unto the woman, What is this that thou hast done? And the woman said, The serpent beguiled me, and I did eat.

Talk about passing the buck.

And the LORD God said unto the serpent, Because thou hast done this, thou art cursed above all cattle, and above every beast of the field; upon thy belly shalt thou go, and dust shalt thou eat all the days of thy life.

Then, as a punishment for their disobedience, he kicks Adam and Eve out of the garden of Eden, and sends them down into a harsh world to toil and suffer and eventually die. It is such a clever little tale, if you think about it. It offers you a single answer to so many things that have been deeply perplexing to people throughout the ages. Why do women bring forth children in pain? Why must people work so hard to feed themselves? Why do people wear clothes? What makes them ashamed of being naked? Why does everyone eventually die? If the world in which you were struggling for existence brought these troublesome questions to mind, you can see how tempting the tale would be. It even tells you why serpents crawl on their bellies. Because Adam and Eve broke God's commandment. And who led them into that world-altering act? Why, the serpent, of course, that subtle tempter. And why did the serpent do it? Because I had entered into the sinuous creature to sibilate softly into Eve's ear.

And so all human beings, forever after, are tainted with sin. Every innocent little babe, from the moment it is born into this world, is condemned to suffer the same grievous punishments that God inflicted upon Adam and Eve.

Does that make any sense to you? Does it sound at all reasonable?

Well, apparently not everyone thought so. Some

groups could not believe that a benevolent God would act so perversely. The tale, they assumed, must be holding some deeper meaning. They took a closer look, with their own eyes, and what did they find? Oh, yes.

There it was. How could they have missed it?

What they uncovered is still lurking among the shifting shadows of history. It has been hushed up for many centuries now by a number of noted individuals who simply did not like it. With a grim determination to keep it suppressed, they branded it *heretical*, for not only did it let me off the hook. It made a hero of me. Ha!

Can you believe that? No? Then take another look.

8

Now the serpent was a subtle counselor. One day, many years ago, Adam and Eve were outside the garden, sitting under a lone tree. The serpent made its way toward them along one of its leafless branches. Hanging sinuously down between them, it swiveled its head, looking at each of them. "Any other questionsss?"

"Hey!" said Adam. "Good to see you again. A lot's been happening, as you said it would. But, wow, so confusing! What's going on here?"

The serpent's head swiveled again.

Eve was gazing at Adam now. She was smiling, with a sensuously satisfied look.

"Yesss," said the serpent. "I see much has happened."

"Well," said Adam. "It all took place just the way you said it would. We ate the fruit, as you advised, and the Old One came down and gave us hell."

"Of courssse," said the serpent. "You upset his

plans. You were supposed to stay as innocent as new-born babies. Or should I say as ignorant?" As it hung there by its tail from the branch above them, its head began to nod again, with a swaying motion, insinuating certainty.

"So, anyway, here we are," Adam said. "What happens next?"

"You journey forth, on your own now," said the serpent.

"To where?" Adam wrinkled his brow, looking confused.

The serpent hissssed softly at the sight. "To the knowledge that would otherwise have been kept from you."

"Hmmm," said Adam. "How long a journey?"

"No more than a lifetime," said the serpent.

"A lifetime." The new word seemed to trouble Adam. "So what the Old One told us was the truth? We've lost more than just the garden?"

"And gained more than you have lost," the serpent said. "Your garden world was designed to be such a cheerful little place, so carefully constructed, just for you, with every flower commanded to smile brightly whenever you appeared. It was all put together to keep you distracted from becoming aware of your deplorable ignorance."

"Yes," said Eve, watching the serpent. "It was true, what you said."

"Just think for a moment of what you have gained by eating of the fruit." The serpent's head, with bead-brightened eyes, began swaying again. "Your thoughts and feelings are free to move now beyond the confines of this little, this very little garden. You have brought forth another sun into the sky that will shine for you upon the new world you are now free to create for yourselves. And, oh, what a world it will be, composed of beautiful forms and feelings you will bring forth from within yourselves. They will radiate their own brilliance across and even beyond your lifetime. You will call them works of art."

"Lifetime," Adam echoed somberly again. "Everything has its costs, though, doesn't it?"

"Yesss," said the serpent. "You can forget about the never-ending primrose path you were on. But it's all a matter of perspective, isn't it? Something better awaits you now, something more interesting, and certainly more profound." As its head slowly swiveled back and forth again, the serpent's red tongue flicked out once at each of them. "Across every moment of your now uncertain lifetimes, you will carry with you the possibility of experiencing an exquisite joy, the feeling of having each other, and of knowing each other, with a depth and an intensity you would never have found in your pathetically pleasant little garden." The serpent stopped swaying. "What awaits you now is nothing less than the entire world. Look there, before you. See where it lies."

"Why are you doing this?" Adam said. "I don't understand why you're doing this."

"It's obvious, isn't it?" said the serpent. "Who else would have told you?"

"But why are you?" Adam insisted.

The serpent tried to shrug, but didn't bring it off. "The truth is, I like you two. There is something about you. And when I saw how completely the deck had been stacked against you, and that you didn't have an inkling, not a single suspicion, I took pity upon you and offered my help. Fortunately, you took it. And now you are free. The world still awaits you, and all that you can do with it."

"Fair enough," Adam said. "And we thank you for your help." He rose then and held out his hand to Eve.

The serpent watched as their two hands touched and they smiled to each other from somewhere more deeply within themselves. Then they turned and began to walk together down the pathway that led into the midst of the wilderness they could see stretching out below them.

As they were disappearing into the distance, the serpent curled the corners of its mouth up into a reptilian smile.

9

I rather like my version of the Eden tale. I really do. Probably because it nudges up so much closer to the truth. But I would certainly not limit you just to my account. I could be biased, after all. Cherry-picking my evidence. And so I suggest that we glance at one or two of the other variations that were also making the rounds in those early days. Like the account, say, of that early Gnostic sect, the Ophites, or serpent worshipers.

Such an enticing name. May it lure you on now. Especially if you already believe that all snakes are symbols of evil.

The Ophites, taking their own look, were convinced that the serpent in the garden of Eden was actually a positive presence. Who, after all, had awakened Adam and Eve to the degrading ignorance in which they were being kept? If the Eden tale, they wondered, had misled so many people about the serpent, then what about the God who appeared there? After opening their eyes and reconsidering the evidence that lay before them, and with a bit of urging from me, of course, they came up with an answer that would turn the tale on its head. Well, at least for a while. They reached the conclusion that the Eden tale must be about some other god. It was clearly a less than benevolent god, indeed a rather deplorable figure.

They looked more closely into other accounts, and there was the same god, committing or condoning terrible acts, and bragging about his powers. 'I form the light, and create darkness: I make peace, and create evil." What kind of god would brag about bringing evil into this world, the very world that he also claimed to have created? "I have made the earth, and created man upon it." So be it, said the Gnostics. And with the force of a lightning bolt, they split their image of God in two. This was obviously a lesser god, far below the highest God they sought in their worship. This god was a pathetic figure, possessing too many of the failings to be found in human nature, a jealous god who wanted to lord it over human beings. He would keep them in their lowly place by denying them knowledge. As the creator of evil and strife in the world, this god did not deserve to be worshiped. They called him a *Demiurge* and condemned the world he had created. It was an awkward, blundering creation, a repugnant world of matter that, by its very nature, corrupted the spirit.

But, like tin cans tied to the tail of a snake, the Gnostic view arrived with some complicated clatterings about our old problem, the origin of evil. If this world, with all of its obvious defects, was a botched job by some inferior power, if all matter is to be viewed as a corrupting influence upon the spirit, if sin is to be found in the very nature of things, then how could any mere mortal escape its effects? How, indeed, could any individual be condemned for committing a sinful act? Oh, but that view was simply unacceptable. Think of the consequences. Chaos would surely come again. It struck me at the time as such a delightful dilemma. I took particular pleasure in watching so many noted individuals wiggle and squirm, like worms on a fishhook, to get off that penetrating point.

Enter our next tale-teller, Manichaeus, another Persian prophet. This one lived in the third century AD. (Yes, I know.) Manichaeus claimed to have the answer to all such questions still troubling people throughout the known world. Zoroastrians, Gnostics, Buddhists, Christians, what have you. He would bring them all together, into harmony, under one universal religion.

They would all become Manichaeans. Ha!

Manichaeus, to his credit, did offer them a compelling tale. Judge for yourself. And see, by the way, if any of its bits and pieces sound at all familiar to you. But I caution you. Do not get too distracted here. You could easily lose sight of me.

Imagine Light and Darkness as separate realms, existing apart from each other. Light is a God-ruled spiritual realm of order and peace, while Darkness is an evil place of matter, churning with hatred and violence. These distinctive settings remain apart until the powers within Darkness, moving about their realm, come to their outermost boundary, and there, for the first time, perceive Light. The sight overwhelms them. It fills them with envy, and arouses in them the desire to enter into and take over the realm of Light. Attacking with all the fury possessed by evil forces, Darkness, for the first time, captures and mixes itself in with part of the Light.

God then responds to the vicious onslaught by devising a plan to redeem the lost Light. He begins by creating the visible world, the one you find yourself in, out of the unholy mixture, with the intention of later dissolving the evil part—in other words, wiping out your physical world—and returning the realm of Light to its pure, undefiled state. And so, in this account, we have God, and not some Demiurge, bringing forth a corrupted world—with good intentions, of course.

However, the powers within the realm of Darkness are determined to keep the Light they have captured. Out of the now corrupted mixture of Light and matter, they fashion what they believe will be a more durable combination by creating two new figures, Adam and Eve. How about that for an interesting turn in the plot? And it gets even better, for Eve is now assigned the lecherous task of luring Adam into a sexual union. If she succeeds, it will begin the process of birth. And that will prove to be a darkly clever means to disperse the captured Light among the ensuing inhabitants. As they come forth throughout the world, they will keep the Light from ever being successfully reclaimed by God.

Responding to this new threat, God sends forth a messenger to warn Adam, a messenger who is called Jesus. (Just watch now how my role is usurped here.) Jesus is not able to reach Adam before Eve has her way, and so the evil process commences, presenting God with another challenge. What can he do now?

God makes a counter-move. He has Jesus appear to Adam as, of all things, a serpent! And he has the serpent lead Adam—Where else?—to the tree of knowledge. The serpent then encourages Adam to eat, for, within this matter-corrupted world, there is only one role left now for human beings to play, as God pursues his ultimate goal of reclaiming the Light. Like the Gnostics before him, Manichaeus comes to believe that the ultimate salvation of every human being can be achieved now only through the pursuit of knowledge.

Was that last part a let-down for you? The pursuit of knowledge? How entertaining could that possibly be?

It was a most compelling tale in its day, one that attracted great attention. Manichaeus captured a host of minds with it, both in the East and the West. He spread his vision so successfully that he aroused the jealousy of dominant religious figures in various lands. Being religious, of course, they all denied feeling even a touch of jealousy. That would be below them. Down somewhat closer to my supposed realm.

Manichaeus was also considered dangerous by the political figures in those lands. They were deeply troubled by the rapidly growing numbers of his converts. And so jealousy and fear, combining their deadly forces, moved to strike him down. They branded him a heretic, they executed him, and then they began to persecute his followers.

Does that sound at all familiar to you?

*****

Sure it does. I know who you mean.

Am I wrong, Wag? Or did I catch you thinking?

He-he. Maybe you caught me. It must have been those crazy names. Zoroaster. Manichaeus. Where do you keep finding such weird people?

History is full of weird people.

Then why not leave them there, in the past? I mean, they're dead. They're not even alive.

Because we need to understand them, Wag.

Why do we need? What's the point?

What did Santayana say? Those who cannot remember the past are condemned to repeat it.

Not me. I can't remember, and I'll be damned if I'm going to repeat it.

Well, then you are an exception, Wag.

Don't start calling me names.

10

*E*arlier, to prepare the way for both the Gnostics and the Manichaeans, I had also brought forth some particularly provocative ideas among the Greeks. Yes, I said provocative. The kind I like best. My goal was to have the Greeks question one of their most fundamental beliefs: that the world was a place of beauty and order. If you had even the slightest doubt, they claimed, all you had to do was look up at the multitude of heavenly bodies moving in perfect circles around you. Or so, at least, you were told. And what was at the very center of the universe, the focal point of all its magnificent motions? Why, the earth, of course, created by the gods as an ideal home for humanity.

But I would not let everyone simply swallow that obvious misconception. I urged selected individuals to look more closely for themselves at the workings of the world. And when they did, they began asking some disquieting questions. What was that you said about the heavenly bodies? They moved in perfect circles around us? But how, then, would you explain the changes we all can see in lunar eclipses of the sun? During some eclipses, the moon completely covers the face of the sun.

At other times, a ring of sunlight can be seen around the edge of the moon. There is no denying what that means. The distance between the sun and the moon must be varying. But how could that be if everything is moving in perfect circles?

What a wonderfully thoughtful period it was! Just look at Lucretius and his dazzling ideas. I am still basking in their warm glow. It was "sheer folly," he said, to think of the world being made for humankind by some divine power, "so great are the defects with which it is encumbered." Plato also puzzled over those defects and then presented his own belief, an early version of the Gnostic view, that the world was constructed by inferior powers who had botched things up a bit. But then he had a remarkable insight for that early time. He came to believe that sin and disorder and death should all be viewed as persisting traces, as leftovers, if you will, of the chaos out of which everything was created. It was another bold step in the right direction. But it faded with his passing, and has all but disappeared now into the darkening shadows of ancient history.

Why had Manichaeus shifted the role of serpent away from me? Because he now wanted the serpent to be viewed as coming from God. What a laugh. Ha! What an *injustice*. And he did not want to blame God for the presence of evil in God's created world. So he simply envisioned another source. The powers of Darkness, envying the Light, had broken out of their unenlightened realm and had brought evil both to the world at large and into the nature of each human being. That, of course, includes you. A bit of Darkness. A bit of Light. Stir well, and there you are, a perpetuating part of that corrupted mixture.

Ah, but can you see what that vision implies? The heavy cost that rides along with it? If the visible world is now looked upon as a place of corruption, rather than a setting of beauty and order, and if even God now has to struggle against the encroaching forces of evil, where, then, does that leave every human being who is caught up in such a world? As mere mortals, what chance would they have? Since they had been swept up in a cosmic battle far beyond their control, how, then, could they be blamed for anything sinful in this world?

"I will show you how," said Augustine, after looking inside himself. And what had he discovered now, in the fourth century AD, that no one else before him had ever seen? Why, there it was, the presence of a new sin, as plain as the throbbing bit of flesh that rose up by itself before him. Well, he concluded, with a classic illogicality, if I can find that sin within my own nature, then it must exist within every human being. But what was the source of this insidious evil? Where had it first arisen? Augustine, offering his introverted answer, fixed his eye firmly on me. God had nothing to do with evil. It was all my fault, with a little help from that ungrateful couple in the Garden of Eden.

And so my reputation was to suffer again. After a briefly improved image among the Gnostics, I teetered now on the edge of an even steeper decline.

Into original sin.

*****

Nothing original about sin. It's been around a long time.

True, Wag. But many people have wondered when it first appeared here on earth.

You mean, the very first time ever? Is that what you're saying here?

Yes, the very first time ever.

Well, I know when I first did it.

Your first sin? Tell me, Wag.

I was only twelve at the time. But that didn't stop me. I was copying down a page of words somebody was saying. I was supposed to be copying only what was said. But then, I don't know, it just happened. I put in some of my own words. Changed what I was copying. Tried to spruce it up a bit.

And that was it? Your first sin? That does not sound very sinful, Wag.

Not to you maybe. But in my line of work, that's the worst sin there is.

Well, I have to admire your standards. They do, indeed, please me, Wag. You are, after all, writing down the story of my life.

I only did it once before. Never again.

But across all those many years of writing, you must at least have been tempted at times.

Only when I got really bored. Bored to tears. By what I was writing.

And if you find my story boring now? Will you be tempted again?

That's up to you then, isn't it? Just be sure you don't bore me to tears.

But how can I be sure, Wag?

You know what a real sin would be? What if one of my tears plopped? I mean, right down on the page here, the one lying open in front of me?

What an inky mess that would make. Right there in the middle of your story.

Not very much of a sin, Wag. And certainly not an original one. I can already tell where you are headed here.

Who said headed? I'm not headed.

What makes me think of a little gray mouse now, running around a black keyboard? And why does a printer come to mind here? With a stack of clean white pages in it.

You're trying to make me cry, aren't you?

11

Original sin. What a profound distortion.

Should I ask here if you have ever taken a good look at the Eden tale? I mean, a really close look. If you had, it might have surprised you, for there is no mention of original sin. You will not even find *sin* in the tale. And who said it was an apple on the tree of knowledge? There is no *temptation*, no *seduction*, no *fall of man*. Why, then, did Augustine drag his new sin into the tale? Because he wanted to discredit both the Gnostics and the Manichaeans, who were saying that the serpent was a positive presence in the garden. The Manichaeans, you might remember, had viewed the serpent as a messenger from God. Augustine, however, had other ideas.

And, unfortunately, other feelings. Throughout his entire lifetime, but especially during his teens and twenties, Augustine struggled with "the disease of the flesh" that he believed was tainting his existence. The "pestilent desires" and the "insatiable lust" that he found within his own nature were deeply troubling urges that lay, he felt, beyond his own willful control. What, then, he wondered, was their source? Could it possibly be a personal weakness? Of course not, he convinced himself. Since he had not chosen to have such strong sexual urges, they must have been placed there by his creator. But why would his beloved creator bedevil him in that way? He could come up with only one answer. Augustine did not believe that sexual desire was *natural*. Nor was death a natural part of life. Obviously, he said, they are punishments inflicted upon all of us by God. As part of Adam and Eve's punishment for breaking his commandment, God must have instilled an uncontrollable lust in their natures, as living proof of their fall from grace. And, because they are humanity's original parents, it has been passed on, like a genetic defect, to every human being on earth.

Astonishing, if you think about it. Such an all-encompassing degradation of human nature, fabricated by one individual responding to the natural workings of his own body. The Eden tale, Augustine now announced, was not about the search for knowledge. The Gnostics and the Manichaeans were simply mistaken. The emphasis needed to be shifted back to where it belonged, on the state of sin into which all human beings had fallen, and on sinuous me, the subtle tempter. Once again, I was branded the source of all evil.

Original sin. The loss of Eden. Sexual desire and death as part of God's wrathful punishment. There is a troublesome problem I am faced with here, for the more I talk about these ideas, the more people get caught up in them. It is like seeding an empty brain.

Anything scattered there will grow. So understand this. They are *ridiculous* ideas. Is there any way I can express that more clearly?

Even during Augustine's life, a host of respected thinkers considered Augustine's radical new ideas to be absurd, and there were those who did not hesitate to argue openly with him. Just look at Pelagius, or Julian of Eclanum. What? Never heard of them? Can you imagine why? A just God, they declared, would not punish all human beings, condemning everyone on earth to death, for the sin committed by one man.

That idea simply did not sound right to them. They looked around for themselves and reached their own conclusions. Death was a natural part of all life. And, whatever Adam's transgression might have been, the world they saw had not been corrupted by sin.

It is said that God allows evil to exist in the universe because, with his omnipotence, he can bring forth good even out of evil. My experience of the world, across the ages, has convinced me that believing in a superior god all too often leads to evil being brought forth out of good. With a deep commitment to his own "most omnipotent" God, Augustine took a classical world in which human beings were generally admired as creatures of reason, possessing free will and living in dignity, and he transformed that world into a seething cauldron of sin and sex, which boiled over afterwards, and spread out in all directions, corrupting everything it touched.

Just look, if you will, at what happened to Pan, one of the more likeable figures in the classical world. Pan was a nature god who joyfully reigned over the countryside and the shepherds watching their flocks.

Pan invented the shepherd's pipes, fashioning them out of reeds. He played the pipes so beautifully that, in a contest with Apollo, who played the lyre, the prize was given to Pan. Viewed as a force existing in nature, this pleasure-seeking figure was also considered the god of sexual desire. Oh, oh. Before Augustine, the Greeks looked on sex as a creative force. Yes, it could also be destructive, but the Greeks nevertheless recognized the full range of its potential. And they had never thought of Pan as being in any way suggestive of Augustine's devil. But Pan was depicted as having the horns and the hoofs of a lusty goat. His body was hairy. His face, with a beard, had an impish expression. And, yes, he was the god of sexual desire. Before Augustine appeared on the scene, not a single artist had attempted to draw a picture of me. But after Augustine associated sex with evil, artistic portrayals of me began to appear. And who did I look like? Why, Pan, of course.

What a handy image it proved to be for anyone sadly lacking in.... Well, take a moment here, and try to imagine what.

*****

I didn't like that last chapter much.

Really, Wag? What was it that troubled you?

What you said about the classical world. It just wasn't like that.

Tell me, then, Wag. What was it like?

It wasn't a flesh-pot of sex and sin. Everybody kept their clothes on. And it was a lot more exciting than all that stuff you just said about it.

Interesting. But how do you know that?

That movie I saw. It was actually made in Rome. Nothing boring there, believe me. And what about that chariot race! It was all so exciting, everything I saw! Nothing at all like you said.

Well, Wag, the past is often seen through many different eyes.

What do you mean? My eyes aren't different. One on each side of my nose. Like all those people who saw that movie. And they all thought it was pretty special.

What are you trying to tell me, Wag?

Well, your story so far. What can I say? It's not exactly a chariot race.

How would you describe it, then?

More like a tractor pull, perhaps. Lead weights on a skid board. Are you trying for some kind of record?

Heavy, Wag. But what are you saying? That people might enjoy here a touch of Hollywood?

Now you're talking! Where's my quill? The big one, with the egret feather.

12

Our grave journey toward the true source of all evil in this world apparently is going to take us now through the middle of an amusement park.

The new image I had been given, with horns and hoofs and a hairy body, proved to be quite entertaining, indeed, especially among the common crowd. I was turned into a comic-book character who started popping up all over the place. I began to be ridiculed wherever I appeared, as a dull-witted figure who was out-foxed, out-tricked, out-maneuvered by some clever hero or heroine. In one particularly delightful tale, the hero caught me by the nose with a pair of red-hot tongs. It made me roar so loud with pain that I could be heard three miles away. Ha ha. Very funny. In another tale, a saintly man cut open a bag of lost souls that I was carrying to hell, and he let them all escape.

> Away went the Quaker—Away went the Baker,
> Away went the Friar—that fine fat Ghost,
> Whose marrow Old Nick

Had intended to pick,
Dress'd like a Woodcock, and served on toast!

I was so mad about the loss of my supper that I picked up a huge boulder and threw it at the saintly man's bald pate. After miraculously bouncing off his head, without even breaking the skin, the boulder headed back toward me.

And it curl'd, and it twirled, and it whirl'd in air,
As this great, big stone at a tangent flew!
Just missing his crown, it at last came down
Plump upon Nick's Orthopedical shoe!

And of course I made all the appropriate noises that tickled the fancy of the general audience.

Oh! what a yell and a screech were there!
How did he hop, skip, bellow, and roar!
"Oh dear! oh dear!"

My many appearances increased dramatically as I found myself being broken up into little pieces, atomized into devilets, who were looked to now as the evident cause, not only of every sin committed, but of all discomforts of any kind felt in daily life. I could understand the many supposed evils being attributed to fractured me, the lusting, the blasphemy, what have you, and even some of the questionable actions, like gambling and drinking. But it got to the point where I had become the scapegoat lurking behind everything, however trivial, that struck anyone as somehow not quite right. Dancing? Hmmm. Look at how she moves. Hunting? Look at the glint in his eyes. Courtiers? What arrogant sneers. And what about those brightly colored pantaloons? Do you see that horse getting wild under its rider? Do you feel qualmish after you overeat? Does your hand feel chilly when you expose it to the winter wind? Do you feel lazy in the morning? I could be found everywhere people looked, and in every unpleasant feeling they had. And I could be heard everywhere, too, as people claimed that I was whispering evil thoughts to them, in the rustling of their clothes, the scratching of their skin. At the height of this madness, some dim-witted authority named Borrhaus, as I recall, took great pains to calculate the number of devils existing in this world. It had to be, he declared with irrefutable certainty, at least 2,665,866,746,664.

These all-encompassing portrayals of me, I have to admit, were a most effective distraction, further suppressing the revelation of my true nature. People were attracted now to other issues they found more personally relevant. Earlier, God had been let off the hook when I was branded the one who had brought evil into this world. Now, human beings had an excuse for all their own sinful acts as the responsibility was shifted away from them and heavily dropped, like a shower of anvils, upon each and every representation of me. "The Devil." "It was the Devil." "The Devil made me do it." And what, you may ask, did I make them do most often? Why, to succumb, time after time, to that most bedeviling of all natural urges. It was the Augustinian touch again. It never fails. Just take a look, inside yourself, and there it is. The Devil's calling card. Sexual desire. Can you see how effectively that hindered their thoughts from reaching out, unencumbered, to wherever they might go? It sharply focused their attention now, not on my primary role in their lives, but on the physical workings of their own bodies, as though something evil had touched them and corrupted their natures. Suddenly, their minds were flooded with guilt. It was a clever diversion, this warping of reality, but all such diversions come with a cost. And this one also proved to be heavy, indeed.

If sexual desire was branded a corruption, then anything, or anyone, arousing that desire could be looked upon as sinful. What a conveniently useful thought that was, at least for half of humanity. All males were now able, indeed delighted, to unload their own guilt upon the other half of humanity, the gentler sex. Men became the victims of women, the arousers. Women were even charged, by men, of course, with corrupting some of the occupants of heaven. A sizeable group of angels supposedly looked upon the fair and beautiful daughters of men and lusted after them. When the angels coupled with them, the women gave birth to evil giants, who were known to have walked upon the early earth. Women who dressed up or used cosmetics to enhance their allurements artificially were, supposedly just like me, also liars and deceiving creatures. It was further claimed that I myself could appear in the form of a beautiful woman to tempt men into lustful acts. Alluring women were looked at now with deep suspicion, if not revulsion.

Troubled, as they have always been, by the urges arising within their own bodies, men have struggled across the ages to resist, or even deny, the commanding presence that nature has given women within their lives.

Stand with me here, for a moment, on this street in Teheran, and let us watch that young Muslim woman walking past in the late afternoon. Chador-clad, her eyes barely visible through the narrow opening in the cloth, she makes her way along the sidewalk like a small black cloud trying to sneak across the sky, for a group of young, loud-talking men have gathered on the corner ahead. With her head bowed and her eyes fixed on the ground before her, she moves carefully past them, controlling the motions of her body to keep its presence completely hidden beneath its black covering. The young men glance at her as she passes. A muted remark is made, and then she hears their raucous laughter behind her.

Later, the young men disperse. One of them, who owns the shop on the corner where they had gathered, lingers, glancing up at the darkening sky, wondering when it will start to rain. It will drive his customers away again, as it always did. He stands there on the sidewalk outside his shop, taking in the swarms of people moving up and down the street. When he feels the first drop of rain, he looks up censoriously at the sky. As the black clouds overhead begin to unveil themselves and let fall their nurturing showers onto the waiting earth, his face twitches with irritation.

Was that a bit too subtle, perhaps?

Step down a level, then, and join me in that cold, barely furnished, twelfth-century cell, where I watched Saint Dominic Loricatus lacerate his body day and night with a pair of scourges, flagellating his flesh to keep its ever-present lustings under control. Determined to show his body who was boss, he struggled to keep his thoughts entirely free of flesh.

But all he learned, much to his dismay, was that his body had other ideas.

Would you like to know what Jack the Ripper was after? Walk with me, then, through this damp and darkening evening in the Evil Quarter Mile of Whitechapel, London. The lamplighter, making his way along the rough stones of the street, lifts his long pole as the fog moves in and curls around the lamp he lights, leaving it a dull, vaporous glow that barely reaches the ground. A woman stops beneath the lamp, seeking a moment's respite from the chilling presence of some vague evil that she senses is following her, an unseen shadow being shaped into existence out of the tar-pit of night.

She gasps as a man suddenly looms before her out of the fog, and then, with relief, puts her hand on her bosom and smiles at the stranger, a gentleman, clearly, and such a pleasant face. Her eyes sparkle in anticipation as she sizes him up. She could charge him a pretty penny, she thinks. It's going to be her lucky night after all.

Later, as she lies there on the ground in the dark and grimy court she has led him into for his moment of paid pleasure, he straddles her body and lifts her skirts. But her widened eyes no longer sparkle at him as the fog now licks at their startled, unblinking stare. Her throat is slit open from ear to ear, the knife cutting so deep that it has nicked her spine. She was right, in one sense, about its being her lucky night, for she would not have to watch what he was about to do to her.

With the bloody knife still in his left hand, he bares the bottom half of her body, and then, deftly, draws the knife across the middle of her stomach, laying it open. From the middle of that cut, he slices again, downward this time, until he is able, with additional trimmings, to fold back two large flaps of flesh, revealing her intestines. Plunging his right hand into the coilings, he pulls out the intestines, slippery and steaming now in the cold night air, cutting them loose wherever they cling to the interior, and throwing them to the side above her shoulder. And there, finally exposed to his view, are the parts that he will remove and carry away, the secrets of a Circe, whose sensuous touch can turn grown men into grunting swine. The flesh-enfolded signifiers of her sex: her vagina, her uterus, and her ovaries.

It wasn't just a senseless hacking away. He tried very methodically with his victims to cut out the female parts of their bodies, leaving a grossly mutilated, but essentially sexless form of flesh, at least in his mind's eye, maniacally distorted as it was. Sinuously stalking some pathetic prostitute through the dark and foggy streets of London, it was ultimately escape that he was seeking from the unrelenting, inescapable urges of his own bedeviling body. He was trying, with desperate dementia, to deprive her of her capacity to turn him on, and thus to assert her dominance over him, simply because of the way she was physically constructed.

It is painful to think of how many lives have been distorted since Augustine turned sex into a sin. And how many people went to such sad extremes to control the natural urges of their bodies. When I appeared in feminine guise to Saint Paphnutius, the anchorite, or so the tale goes, the only way he was able to resist my seductive charms was to stick his hands into the fierce flames of a fire burning in his cell. The tale, of course, can be looked at with a healthy dose of disbelief. But not so with that other noted saint, Rose of Lima, who was so troubled by her own attractive appearance that she actually rubbed quicklime on her beautiful face and tragically burnt it off. Or, indeed, with Origen, who later became a deeply respected father of the church. As a young man, he struggled with the sexual desire he could feel burning within his own body, but he was not able to bring it under control. What could he do? There was only one choice. He castrated himself.

Pause here for just a moment, and think about it. What compelled these two individuals, male and female, to condemn and mutilate the natural workings of their own bodies? It had to be a deep belief. But was it their own? Or something spoon-fed to them by someone else?

Keep your wits about you now, for we are approaching another mind-fettering fence. Having made our way past that Augustinian condemnation of sexual desire, what we find now, posted ahead, is a much larger NO TRESPASSING sign.

Various noted figures, across the ages, have struggled mightily to keep you from going any further, for they were fearful of what you might discover beyond the borders of their own beliefs. But look beyond that intimidating fence, and you will get a glimpse of what awaits you there, with its ancient warning label still in place.

Forbidden knowledge.

*****

Forbidden knowledge. I know what you mean.

Tell me, Wag. What do I mean?

Well, there are some things people just shouldn't see.

Like what, Wag? Give me an example.

Like the inside of that woman, when you opened her up. All that blood, and the body parts. Those should be private parts. No peeking allowed.

But what if you were a doctor, say? Or, better still, a surgeon? Or even Michelangelo, Wag? Did you know that, in his day, he, too, turned to watching corpses be cut open? He wanted to see how they were constructed inside. It helped him, he claimed, to craft more accurately some of his most famous sculptures.

That's a good example, isn't it?

Yes, Wag. I think it is.

No, I mean of forbidden knowledge. Kind of creepy, isn't it? Wanting to do that? Just to make a statue?

Where would you draw the line, Wag? At what point should knowledge become forbidden?

I don't think I can spell it out. Find the right words, I mean. But I'd sure know it when I see it.

The same thing, as I recall, has been said about pornography.

Who said it? Do you know?

A number of well-known people, Wag.

Were they smart people? Did they know a lot?

Yes, indeed, Wag. Highly Intelligent. A good many of them were in the field of law, including a Justice of the Supreme Court.

Puts me in good company, doesn't it?

Careful there, Wag. Such a big grin. How can you write with your eyes squeezed close?

13

Forbidden knowledge. It is one of the world's oldest tales, with a thousand ways of telling it. Would you like to hear a version or two? Take a peek at the forbidden parts? What is it that attracts so many people to anything labeled *forbidden?* And why do so many other people work so hard to stick that label on everything beyond their grasp? Are you acquainted at all with any of those label stickers? Do you think they are clear enough within themselves about why they do it with such determination? By choice, is it? By nature? Or with a spoon stuck in their mouth?

Back, then, to those tales I mentioned. And, as we delve more deeply into this realm, you can see if your thoughts about what we find there are, indeed, your own.

We begin with an ancient Babylonian account. An angel named Asael goes against God's will by bringing down some heavenly secrets and making them known to human beings. Can you guess what happens then to Asael's reputation? Even though the secrets he revealed were heavenly, they are twisted into ones that bring evil into the world. Asael teaches human beings how to dig up and to refine the metals that are in the earth, but only to make breastplates out of bronze and swords out of iron.

He shows them how to fashion gold and silver, but only to make adornments for women. He reveals to women the secret mysteries of hair-dyes and eye shadows. It is all, of course, forbidden knowledge, leading men to warfare, and women to artificial allurements. God then charges Asael with having brought all evil into the world, and he punishes Asael by banishing him from heaven and casting him down into total darkness, never to see the light again.

Does it sound at all familiar to you, this ancient Babylonian tale? Another thief of heavenly knowledge was Prometheus, whose name meant "forethought." He had a brother named Epimetheus, "afterthought." The two of them were given the task by Zeus to create mankind and the other living creatures on earth. Proceeding directly to the job, Prometheus scooped up a batch of clay, and, after mixing in a little water, he stood there, hefting the glob in his hand until, with a bit of inspired forethought, he brought the gods to mind as models. Then he molded the material into a human being. Epimetheus, after watching him, then took some clay, and he shaped it into an animal. Every time that Prometheus gave a distinctive trait to human beings, Epimetheus, as an afterthought, gave the same trait to the animals.

Prometheus, however, wanted his creations to be superior to the animals, and so he gave human beings a very special gift. He brought down fire for them from the heavens. It proved to be a most useful gift, for it allowed them to warm themselves, to cook their food, and to craft the materials of their world into tools, medicines, and a host of other helpful things. But the Olympian gods were opposed to giving heavenly fire to human beings, and so Zeus took it back.

Prometheus then became a heavenly rebel. Going against the will of Zeus, he stole the fire and returned it to the human inhabitants of earth. Did I mention, by the way, that Prometheus, with his forethought, was looked on as a figure possessing wisdom? Zeus, however, was not at all pleased with this rebellious act. He had Prometheus chained to the side of a mountain, where an eagle arrived every day and fed upon his liver.

As a punishment to human beings—although I do not see why they deserved it—Zeus had Hephaestus take some more clay and shape it into Pandora, the first woman. An interesting punishment. The creation of a woman. Before sending her down to earth, Zeus gave Pandora a special box, and he told her never, but never to open it. Talk about setting someone up. It did not take long, as you might guess, for her curiosity to get the better of her. She opened the box, and out came all of the ills and sins that would spread like a plague throughout humankind. And so the first created woman on earth, in this classical tale, is responsible for bringing all evil into this world, because she disobeyed the word of Zeus.

And then, of course, there is the serpent who leads Eve to heavenly knowledge. Eve and Pandora. Sisters in sin. Perhaps the separate tales of these two original woman should have been combined into one. I can easily imagine them sitting together in an idyllic garden on the slopes of Mount Olympus, being warned by God / Zeus never, but never to take one of the apples out of that box, or even to touch one. If they do, something terrible will happen. When their curiosity overcomes them, Pandora lifts the lid, Eve reaches in, and the world is forever messed up, along with their reputations. Ha!

People will do anything to hide their own ignorance, particularly from themselves. Perhaps that accounts for why the pursuit of knowledge, throughout human history, has so often been twisted into something evil. It would not be long before these tales began to be used to condemn anyone who displayed an irresistible curiosity. What, after all, was *forbidden knowledge?* It was everything that God intended to keep beyond the limits of human awareness. With that intimidating thought in mind, people reacted accordingly to anyone attempting to go beyond those limits. Such a foolish step was all too often branded a sinful act of pride, or arrogance, or excessive ambition, dangerous traits that were purposefully selected to recall early portrayals of evil me. I was the heavenly rebel who was punished for trying to rise above his God-assigned place in the hierarchy of heaven. Among certain Florentine painters, I was even pictured as being dressed in the academic robes of a professor. Intellectual curiosity running rampant became a sure sign of someone being in league with me, practicing the black arts to delve more deeply into the mysteries of nature. And who better to illustrate this deadly compact than Doctor Faust, the famous philosopher, who sold me his soul in exchange for the use of my dark powers to gain greater knowledge.

If you think such tales are only mythical, and not true accounts of historical figures, then take a closer look at Socrates. Many early Greeks paid lip service to the search for knowledge. It was supposed to be one of their most noble endeavors, ranked right up there with leading a virtuous life. Socrates had said that the unexamined life is not worth living. He was considered to be the wisest man in the world because he knew what he did not know. Think about that. What about you? Do you know what you do not know? And think about how his fellow Athenians reacted to him for looking more deeply into every claimed truth. He had even questioned the dubious existence of their revered gods. People do not take kindly to anyone who shows them how much they do not know. In recognition of his capacity to disrupt their unquestioned truths, they handed Socrates a cup of hemlock.

And what about good old Galileo, the noted Italian astronomer and physicist, who pointed that primitive telescope at the skies to offer his age a more penetrating look into the depths of the universe? When he invited in a few respected individuals from his town one evening and gave them each a turn at the telescope, they concluded that the device had to be a diabolically clever tool for distorting their view of the eternal heavens. In recognition of his keen ability to look beyond the awareness of his peers, they charged him with heresy and brought him before the Inquisition.

And Roger Bacon, the English scientist? He is one of my personal favorites. I can remember that time when I was seated in the audience at the University of

Paris, encouraging him on, as he presented some of his experiments with light. There was a rumor in the air that Bacon had been taught by the Devil to manipulate mathematical symbols. Those symbols gave him the power to uncover hidden mysteries about his world. How else could he actually take a ray of white light and turn it into all the colors of the rainbow? When Bacon first used a prism to project those colors upon a screen before the audience at the university, they found the sight so shocking that they fled in terror from his presence, and then condemned him afterwards for being in league with me. He was thrown into prison, with his very life in jeopardy.

Oh, ye of little learning.

Such reactions were nothing new to me, for I have encountered them in every age across a large part of the history that I have helped to unfold in the Western world. Time and again, I have had to find a way around or across the same entrenched belief, that the human mind was simply too feeble to understand the nature and the workings of this world. Such knowledge was considered to be far beyond the limits of human comprehension. That, apparently, was what God had intended. From that stifling perspective, the quest for knowledge beyond current awareness was strongly condemned as sinful, as were all curious individuals foolish enough to resist God's will. As people aimlessly milled around in the darkness closing in their world, they actually struggled to convince themselves that God wished to keep them there. Some God.

Fortunately, they also had me surreptitiously roaming among them. I was always able to find a few key individuals who responded to my urging and became restless. Looking up, they could see above them the clarifying brilliance of a sunny day, and they began to search for a way out of the shadows. The world was such a troublesome place, a thorn-strewn pathway of sweat and suffering that led only to the gates of death. What had brought this all about? They wanted to know what had actually happened.

There was once a man and a woman who lived in a garden in Eden.... The tale, which was easy to understand, appeared to be a fitting explanation, and it was based on an intriguing supposition, that there once must have existed on earth an ideal place created by God for human beings, a perfect setting that was then tragically lost. That supposition, as you might expect, led to some rather obvious questions. Why was it lost? Who was responsible? What had they done? It turned out to be, as we have seen, a rather cleverly constructed little tale, and it served all too well to soothe the burning need in people's minds to find an answer. But there was only one small problem with it.

It never happened.

Stop here for a moment and do something really daring, something that too many other people have shied away from doing. Set your feet firmly on the ground, and insist upon a more plausible premise, a rather obvious one, if you think about it: that there simply never was such an ideal setting on earth. What happens then to that elaborately constructed concept of sin that Augustine had built upon that tale?

As it collapses around you with a dust-raising clatter, you find yourself, when the air clears, standing once again on open ground. With your vision unencumbered now, you should be able to see that

you have not yet found it.
    The source of all evil in this world.

*****

I think I already heard you say that. Two or three times before. Whoever you're talking to is going to get bored. Or should I say more bored?

Have I been boring you, Wag?

Me? Are you serious? It's your life you're telling, isn't it? How could I ever find that boring?

Was that something new, Wag? A touch of sarcasm?

He-he. Maybe a touch. Well, you do keep getting off the track. I liked the Eden story you told. Adam and Eve walking down that road. I wanted you to follow them, see what was up ahead. But then it all comes crashing down, and you leave me standing there, choking on dust. Not much fun, I can tell you.

But then the air clears, and what do you see?

I don't know. I'm still coughing up that dust.

Oh, Wag. You are just trying to be difficult.

Why would I do something like that?

What do I see there, floating like a phantom, hovering over your graying head? That little mouse again, moving around? But it has a wire attached to it. What could that possibly mean? Stop waving your hand, Wag. I already know the answer. Time now to turn the page.

Look, then. I'm turning it. And what a surprise. The dust is all gone. I can see again.

14

*H*ave you ever given any thought to why, at this late date, you are still toting that distorted version of the Eden tale across your life? The cause will likely surprise you, for, if you take the time to trace it back to its source, you will discover that you have not yet stepped out of Augustine's shadow. Were you aware, in other words, that, even today, he is continuing to influence the way your mind works? You are carrying around his quirky reading of the tale, like a cocklebur stuck on the back of your clothes, because that is exactly what he wanted you to do. You are fulfilling one of Augustine's most treasured beliefs. But refrain, if you will, from patting yourself on the back, for this particular belief has turned out to be worse even than his concept of original sin.

Take a moment to wonder here. What could be worse than turning that classical world, once noted for its reason and beauty, into a corrupted flesh-pot of sex and sin?

Well, it had to be something terrible, and indeed it was, for, with one well-aimed thrust, Augustine tried to strike at the very heart of the one opponent he found most threatening, the only one capable of correcting his distortions. And who would that be?

Why, me, of course.

Not only did Augustine want to put his thoughts into your mind. He also wanted to stop you from thinking for yourself. Having thoughts of your own, he came to believe, was a straight and narrow pathway into the depths of sin. Augustine declared that if the human mind was ever set free from the strictures of Augustine's own personal beliefs, it would soon turn wild and wallow in the sinful muck of bodily urges.

Sad, really, when you think about. During his younger years, Augustine was one of the most uninhibited philosophical thinkers of his day. He was willing to question *everything*, including his own sexual peccadillos, which he then turned, unfortunately, into philosophical fodder to feed his own incubating beliefs. He said, at one point, that he "wanted to be as certain about things I could not see as I am certain that seven and three are ten." But certainty is a most elusive goal, and Augustine was deeply discomforted without it. Having confronted the turbulent seas of reality, he was finally driven to seek a refuge, which he found in the calm and enclosed harbor of his newly adopted faith. And then he built a wall across the harbor entrance. Having already declared that his natural bodily urges were a sin, he then moved on to the urgings of his mind. "There is another form of temptation, even more fraught with danger. This is the disease of curiosity....It is this which drives us to try and discover the secrets of nature, those secrets which are beyond our understanding, which can avail us nothing and which man should not wish to learn." His curiosity, which had once awakened his mind, was now branded a "malady," a "vain inquisitiveness dignified with the title of knowledge and science." His earlier "appetite" for knowledge, he now claimed, was fed by "perceptions acquired through the flesh," with "the lust of the eyes" leading the pack.

Augustine's aim was to bring the gropings of your own mind to a screeching halt. There were to be no further reasoned explorations into unknown areas, no seeking after questionable knowledge, no free inquiries into established beliefs. Whatever the question, the Church had the answer. Your role would now become one of passively accepting *his* faith and *his* authority. Like an ice-storm moving through the night, encrusting every branch and twig, Augustine's influence settled upon the land. The search for knowledge grew rigid and unmoving. The world was now viewed through apathetic eyes.

I have always been puzzled by the herd mentality among human beings. Help me out here. What does it do for you? Why are you so willing to see your world through someone else's eyes? Is it laziness, or is it fear? I am aware of that deep-seated need you have to feel that you belong, that you are a part of something larger than yourself, something that gives a sense of form to your otherwise formless life. But do you realize what you are trading away to gain that comforting sense?

Remarkably, Augustine got away with it, and not only during his own lifetime. I have to admit that, when I first noticed him, I looked on Augustine as simply another suppressor, with temporary authority, for I had no foreboding, not the slightest, that his influence would last so very long. By doggedly defending his own preferred belief that I was the true source of all evil, and that my every presence had to be repulsed, he and those following faithfully in his footsteps came very close, during the next *thousand* years, to banishing me from the light of their world. That span of time was given an appropriate name. The Dark Ages.

If you had been paying attention, you would have seen something of consequence that I have just revealed to you about my nature, another brush-stroke in the self-portrait I am painting for you. I am not omniscient. I have never claimed to be. I do have an accumulated memory of what has already happened in this world. And I exist with a full awareness of the present. But I do not know what will happen in the future.

No one does.

15

$\int$ex and sin. Did that hold your interest? No, of course not. I should have known. Not at all graphic enough. But what if I throw in some violence now?

Hands and arms being hacked off? Skulls split open? Decapitation? An arrow piercing an eye-socket?

The 4th and 5th centuries were a tumultuous time of many clashing migrations as various groups moved down out of the frozen north to fight for better lands and lives. The Romans responded by looking down their noses at all of the approaching alien hordes, viewing them dismissively as garbled-talking barbarians. But then larger and larger numbers of these outlying people began to pick away at the fringes of the Roman empire, until it finally started to unravel.

My interest, along with a flickering bit of hope, was raised by the Goths as they made their way south, seeking a warmer climate that would offer them some relief from their hard existence. They were a meandering river of human beings, drawn by the lure of fertile lands and the possessions of an advanced culture. Their goal initially was to be accepted as members of the western empire and have a share in its many benefits. In return for the land they sought within the northern borders of the empire, they offered to serve as a defensive buffer against potential invaders. But the Romans, turning a cold eye upon them, saw only a lower, cruder form of life, wearing the malodorous skins of various dead animals. Their offer was rebuffed, and the conflicts continued.

It was not a very clever response, for another, and more deadly, force was already on the way. The Huns were now moving west out of Asia. They were led by a warrior-king named Attila. He was called the Scourge of God. Ha! Sweeping across the land like ravenous locusts, they destroyed everything in their path, as they gathered unto themselves the material spoils of war.

If it had been left up to the Huns, the knowledge that the Greeks had so impressively accumulated would have been trampled into dust as the hordes made their way further and further south. Recorded knowledge, the treasures of the mind, had little material value in their hungry eyes. They devastated the advanced culture achieved within the Roman Empire.

It was indeed a challenging time for me, as I found myself across these years being attacked from all sides. Having struggled to confront the impositions of all the willful emperors, and determined to resist the persisting influence of Augustine and his loyal followers, I now had to face the piercing war-cries of the Huns.

Rapacious ignorance was on the move, and I was standing directly in its path.

In telling you about these historical happenings, I do realize how brief I have been. But I did not want your interest to lag. I wanted to catch and hold your attention. And I think I did rather well. Hordes of people pouring out of the east. A dire threat to the entire western world. The winds of war sweeping through every city and town, as centuries of accumulated knowledge are trampled under the hooves of their thundering horses. How could you possibly expect anything more dramatic than that?

Ah, yes, the blood and gore I mentioned earlier. You were looking, you say, particularly for that arrow in the eye-socket? I thought you would find that rather entertaining. And here you are, still waiting for it. Authors have a term for that little trick. A hook. It keeps you on the line.

Were you aware that a well-crafted lie can actually open your eyes to the truth? And when it does, do you know what that lie is called? You might try *Hamlet*. Or *Moby-Dick*. Did *Ode on a Grecian Urn* come to mind? *Guernica*? The *Emperor's New Clothes*? *Starry Night*?....

One more dab of paint then, for another revelation.

I can be deceptive, whenever I choose. But only if it keeps you moving toward the truth.

16

$\mathcal{A}$nd where, you ask, might that be?

As I watched the western Roman empire crumbling in upon itself, I was not idly sitting on my hands, for I had begun to look for new opportunities to reclaim the knowledge that was in danger of being lost. It lay scattered now in bits and pieces throughout various lands. My attention was soon caught by a most promising place. It was a barren land of almost endless deserts. But there were so many restless minds in the region, just waiting for me to arrive.

It was time, I decided, to try Arabia.

Do you have a map of the world handy? If you already do, by either choice or chance, what does that reveal about you? And if you do not?

As I entered Arabia, I carried with me a heavy load of apprehensions, having already made my way across so many unfriendly ages—No, I correct myself. They were not just unfriendly. There were too many times when a blood-stained fist was smashed down upon the tabletop, insisting upon conformity. Would that, I wondered, ever change?

Mohammed comes to mind here. Another familiar name? No, not him. Much earlier. Try stepping back now, into Arabia. Mohammed appeared, without doubt, at a propitious moment in history, the beginning of the seventh century, for I could sense a smoldering desire for change among the endlessly bickering tribes scattered throughout the Arabian Peninsula. It would take an unusually strong hand to unite them under one banner. As Mohammed rose to prominence among his people, I watched him with deeply mixed feelings. His hand was indeed strong. But it also gripped something else. A set of beliefs. Personal beliefs.

Mohammed had convinced himself, and was then able to convince others, that he was the last great prophet of the one true God, whose name was Allah. After a number of earlier prophets, such as Abraham and Jesus Christ, who apparently did not quite make the grade, now there was Mohammed, the final one chosen to fulfill God's divine plan for humankind. To achieve that goal, God had sent him revelations by way of the angel Gabriel. Coming after the Old and the New Testaments, these final revelations, it was modestly claimed, would bring religious belief and worship to its ultimate state of perfection on earth. Whose god could possibly top that?

In the eyes of Allah, Mohammed announced, all believers belonged to the same brotherhood (no mention yet of sisterhood), regardless of their social rank, their ethnic origins, their skin color, what have you. Everyone was equal, regardless of his status. What an appealing idea, especially to the downtrodden. (Does that sound at all familiar to you?) It was truly a democratic religion—at least for those who believed in it. And for those who did not? As greater and greater numbers came together to serve under his banner, giving him the force of arms he needed to impose his will, the fist, once again, was smashed down on the tabletop. Mohammed returned to the old game. My god is better than your god.

Do not misunderstand me here. I am not at all questioning his sincerity. I have no problem in recognizing that he was deeply committed to his belief that Allah had singled him out and sent him forth to spread the word throughout the land. Once you are convinced that there is only one true God, and that He has chosen You to fulfill his divine will, just imagine what a sense of direction that gives to your otherwise mundane life. Out goes that debilitating feeling of emptiness. In comes an overwhelming sense of *purpose.*

Driven by that feeling, with his ever-growing army of believers, Mohammed spent the next few years bringing all of Arabia under his control. And then, soon after that glorious achievement, he finally died in 632. Mortally speaking, of course. Certainly not in the eyes of his faithful followers, for the Arab armies swept out now beyond the borders of their land. Inspired by Islam and the spoils of war, they spread with a dizzying speed throughout Syria, Egypt, North Africa, and beyond. They extended their rule across vast areas, reaching from southern Spain to the borders of China, taking over almost half the lands of the entire Christian Roman Empire. They appeared to be unstoppable.

Was I troubled? Of course I was. At least in the

beginning. But as I closely followed their activities, I soon discovered that I had made the right choice. Whenever, in their grand conquests, they encountered a more advanced culture, the caliphs proved, to my great relief, to be respectful of it. Instead of wantonly destroying everything in their path, as the Huns had so indiscriminately done, I had little trouble in getting them to recognize the advanced ways and the accumulated learning of the people they conquered. In greater and greater numbers, the Arabs became aware of me moving among them, excited by my presence now, as I encouraged them to treasure not only the material spoils of war, but also the stores of knowledge that were opening their eyes in new ways to the world around them.

I would have found it even more gratifying, as their eyes opened, if only they had taken a better look at me. But such, alas, was not the case, for they, too, already had their heads filled with old stories borrowed from someone else. There were, of course, a few new twists. There always are, as time passes. I was still the cause of all evil in this world, but I was now called Shaitan. (Does that name sound at all familiar to you?) I was also called Iblis, who was the most evil of all the jinn. The jinn were created by Allah out of smokeless fire, and so were a bit higher in the scheme of things than human beings, who were fashioned out of mud or clay. Unlike the angels, who were created out of light, and so remain forever good, both human beings and the jinn could choose for themselves whether they would worship and obey Allah or not.

When Allah first made Adam and brought him forth before the angels and the jinn, he commanded them all, "Fall prostrate before Adam." But Shaitan refused, disobeying Allah's commandment, for, as a figure created out of fire, he believed he was better than someone made out of clay. It was another of those wonderful games. I am made out of better stuff than you are. So Allah cast out Shaitan because of his pride and his arrogance, including all the jinn who followed his lead, sending them down to earth, where they were left free by Allah to roam the lands, trying to turn human beings away from Allah, until the Day of Judgment.

Yes, I know, you have heard it all before. Same play, but with another new cast now.

Stay with me, though, for here is another twist.

Imagine for a moment that you are Shaitan, or one of the jinn. As you spend your time wandering around the world, what do you think will prove to be your most successful approach in turning human beings to evil? Dangling before them a variety of fleshly temptations? Promising them material wealth and power? As it turned out, it was a much less challenging endeavor. Shaitan and the jinn reaped their best crop of evil by simply distracting human beings, and so making them forget about Allah. At that point, apparently, human nature kicked in.

To counter that approach, Allah sent a series of prophets among the people to remind them of their rightful devotion to Allah, prophets such as Abraham, and Solomon, and Jesus. But in every case, Allah's message was not clearly received. It was all too often twisted by others into something different, fractured and distorted into a variety of mixed messages. And what did that lead to, as it usually does? The appearance of misleading and conflicting sects. Yes, of course, chalk up another old game. I know Allah better than you do. I know what he *really said.*

To correct all the disruptive bickering that arose among them, Allah then brought forth Mohammed, his final prophet, and dictated the Koran to him so that His word would remain forever unchanged among all the inhabitants of this earth.

Nice try. But things did not quite work out as planned.

Before we go on, though, I would like to know if you are open at all to joining a particular group that comes to mind here. Very small, and highly selective. It would burnish your credentials in the eyes of the world. And there is only one requirement for joining. Simply read the Koran and then compare it to the King James Version of the Bible. You would find such beautiful language, in both of the works.

Would you like to know how many members are in that group?

*****

I need a break here. Let's take a break.

What is it now, Wag? Why a break?

All that history I'm scratching down. It makes my eyes feel fuzzy. Like moss on a rock. You know what that is? Maybe if I rolled them around, my eyes, I mean. You think that would help any?

Well, Wag, it may simply be that you are getting on in years.

There's more than one way, you know, to say something mean to me. Especially when I need a break. You've been working me pretty hard.

Wag, I would never knowingly say anything mean to you.

And forget about the years. It's not the years. It's all this old stuff you keep saying. That would make anybody feel tired.

Why would it do that, Wag? I do not understand.

Did you ever have a cat? I bet you didn't.

No, Wag. I never had a cat.

Well, then, you should have seen my cat. When she was a kitten, she would sit there beside me, the longest time, just listening to me, as I scratched away at what I was writing. Then all of a sudden she'd jump down and start running all around the room, scratching up everything she could see. Trying to be like me, I guess. She would climb up my leg, like a tree. Jump all over me. Never hold still. And she never got tired either, did she? But all that scratching and the jumping. After a while it was just too much. And about a year ago now it was. She got too tired, and she died on me. Can you see what I mean now?

A very touching story, Wag. But frankly, no. You still leave me puzzled. What is the connection between your cat and your getting tired now as you write?

Who said there was a connection? There isn't one. Aren't you listening?

Then why did you bring your cat up?

What did you expect me to do? Throw her out when she was a kitten?

No, I mean to explain to me why you get tired writing now.

Well, you wanted to know, didn't you?

And the cat is somehow your explanation?

Now you get it. Good for you. Took you long enough, though, didn't it?

Yes, it did. And I finally see why. So you can turn the page now.

Did you ever have even a pet mouse? I bet you didn't. I had one.

Clever, Wag. But not twice. You have had enough of a break, I believe.

Sure you don't want to hear about my mouse?

17

*D*id you really not notice what I was doing?

I have been tugging at two particular threads that run through the fabric of human existence. One thread has a multitude of knots in it that are tied to all those individuals who wanted to stop human beings from thinking for themselves. And the other thread? Well, in spite of it all, a fair number of those human beings simply did not do what they were told.

With the help of that second thread, I have also been pulling you closer and closer to the goal I have in mind for you. The actual source of evil in this world, and why it has remained so deeply hidden across the sweep of human history.

Have you ever had your hope raised to an unexpectedly great height, only to have it dashed to the ground, and shattered into a thousand bits and pieces? That has happened all too often with me, as it did with the fall of the classical world and its many brilliant achievements. With that in mind, you should be able to guess what awaits us now directly ahead. Of course. Another of those devastating reversals.

First, the hope.

After Mohammed had died, and while the Arab armies were continuing their dramatic conquests, what arose next, as you might expect, if you give any thought to human nature, was a struggle for power among Mohammed's successors. Their petty bickerings and their armed clashes persisted for over a hundred years, until a winner at last emerged among them. Abu al-Abbas, with a strong arm and a stronger will, finally defeated all the others and became the first caliph of the Abbasid dynasty. When he established a new capital for his empire in Bagdad, he set the stage for what would be one of history's most remarkable transitions.

Keeping an open mind here may prove to be quite a challenge for you.

I watched now, with an intensifying pleasure, as the caliphs who succeeded him began to gather unto themselves, like the sweet, fleshy fruit of an overhanging date palm, those scattered bits and pieces of the knowledge that I had been so fearful would be lost. The wide-ranging pursuits into all areas of learning that had once so admirably characterized the Greeks were being taken over now by the Arabs, who began by translating the Greek works they came upon into Arabic texts. As they continued their movements in this new direction, the Arabs, to my great delight, blossomed into one of the most advanced cultures in the known world, with Bagdad remaining a center of learning for a good five hundred years. Yes, my hope was indeed riding high.

Then, of course, the shattering.

A new horde of old ravagers, once again mounting their horses, now appeared in force on the scene. In 1258 Hulagu Khan's Mongols swept in from the east like another plague and entered the city. Bagdad, at the time, had public libraries scattered throughout the city. There were thirty-six of them, as I recall, repositories of learning containing not only the classical knowledge that had been uncovered, but also texts of the many advances the Arabs themselves had achieved in all fields of inquiry. With little awareness, and no regret, the Mongols destroyed it all. Hulagu Khan, by the way, was the grandson of Genghis Khan. A chip off the old block. His devastation of Bagdad, with the rampant looting and the careless burning of its many accumulated treasures, was a terrible time for me as I watched those treasures going up in smoke. Were they about to be scattered to the winds again, and finally lost for all time? With knowledge left hanging so precariously in the balance, what could possibly tip the scales in the right direction this time?

Are you interested at all in ironic twists?

There were many Arabs at this time who had remained in key cities in the other lands their armies had conquered. Not wanting to be cut off from the multitude of mind-expanding books that were available in the libraries existing throughout Bagdad, they had requested and received copies of those works. Many of them had already been translated into Arabic, including almost all of the major Greek texts in philosophy, mathematics, and the sciences. The Arabs still living in those distant places steadily built up their own libraries with the writings of such noted figures as Euclid, Hippocrates, Plato, and Aristotle.

And then the Mongols arrived in Bagdad.

Hold on now. This twist has two more turns.

When Christian forces in 1085 invaded Spain to take back that region from the Arabs, Christian scholars followed in the wake of those forces. And when they entered Toledo, lo and behold, what do you think they discovered there? A treasure trove of learning that they thought had forever been lost to them. Here were most of the major Latin writings of the classical world. But they were all, of course, in Arabic. Ha! With little delay, though, an extensive effort was soon underway, not only to translate the texts back into Latin, but also to send on copies of them to cities scattered far and wide throughout the Western World.

Throw open the doors, and raise the windows! I could feel the fresh air again, fanned by the turning leaves of all those classical works. With the dawning of the twelfth century, people throughout the West were becoming increasingly aware of my presence, and their minds awakened, as though from a slumber. Medieval scholars began crying out for more and more of the classical texts. The task of making copies fell upon monks in a wide variety of settings who patiently and, if the truth be told, rather mindlessly worked to fulfill the need.

It is all too easy to picture one of them, sitting at some worn table, blowing on his cold hands, as he thoughtlessly copies page after page of some old and boring scratchings that hold no interest for him. In truth, however, it was another thrilling time of spreading intellectual activity. Until, that is, the Church took notice of what was happening.

Oh, oh. Trouble ahead.

As we leave the Arabs, I have to give them credit. They were not at all intimidated by the knowledge they discovered in the classical texts. They readily accepted all of the learning they considered useful, and built upon it to higher levels, while filling in the gaps they found within their own intellectual pursuits. Indeed, they showed a keen and open-minded interest in the worth of all knowledge, and particularly in everything associated with Christianity, for they assumed, rather reasonably, I thought, that it would be to their advantage to understand the nature and the beliefs of the people they were increasingly confronting.

But what a pathetic comparison when we turn to the Christian Church. As key members of the Church hierarchy began to look more closely at the new texts that were flowing into their areas, they must have thought that Pandora had returned with her box. There were, oh, so many philosophical and scientific writings that were often in direct conflict with the established beliefs of the Church. But it was too late to stop the flow. Dutifully made copies of these works had already been spread across the landscape. What could possibly be done, then, to stifle the pernicious effect they would have on the minds of the people? Shades of Augustine! Once again, the Church banged its fist upon the tabletop.

These pagan works were now condemned, in the strongest language the Church could find. Do you remember that label they always used? Of course. *Heretical.* So that no one would mistakenly stumble into sin, the Church then focused its efforts on compiling and sending out lists of these heretical works. Hundreds and hundreds of the classical texts, the intellectual treasures of the ancient world, were to be avoided like the plague now by every Christian. Deeply troubled by what it viewed as a major attack upon its authority, an attack that was being fomented by—Who else?—me, the Church became grimly determined to tighten its grip on all inquiring minds. It responded once again, as it usually did, by threatening every individual who did not recognize its authority with the ultimate punishment, eternal damnation.

Ah, but I found it easy to ignore such petty posturing, as I watched the Middle Ages coming to an end.

Stand with me now for a moment at the windy top of this beautifully designed stone tower in Constantinople. Look there, off in the distance, and imagine how the inhabitants must have felt back in 1453 as they watched that overwhelming horde approaching their city, a bedazzling force of 150,000 men, with their spear-tips and sword-points glistening in the sunlight, led by the Turkish Sultan Mohammed II. What a deadly time it was about to become. The city was besieged, and the attack strengthened, until the Turks finally breached its fortifications and rode triumphantly through the streets. As every house was broken into, the looting became an unbridled free-for-all, and many of the inhabitants were exultantly slaughtered. One of the men was even found with a bloody arrow still deeply pierced into his eye-socket.

The city was then made the capital of the Turkish empire.

Fearful of remaining in that now inhospitable setting, many of the scholars quickly packed their belongings and headed west, fleeing in great numbers to cities and towns they found more welcoming along the way. And in the end it all led to—Can you guess?—that final ironic twist I mentioned. Since they had carried with them out of Constantinople their most treasured texts, these scholars now became an enticing influence, further arousing, and more widely spreading, curiosity about the classical knowledge that the Church had been trying so desperately to stifle throughout the entire Western world.

What a wonderfully dramatic time! It was my turn now to be unstoppable. So keep your eyes open, and watch closely, for that world is about to undergo another remarkable transformation.

I hesitate here, if only for a moment. Did you find my account at all entertaining?

What about that one image? Surely, that must have caught your eye? I could tell you were still looking for it.

*****

That was kind of mean, wasn't it?

What, Wag? What now?

What you said about all those monks making copies of books.

I said they did it mindlessly, Wag. Did you think that was mean?

Of course it was, if you want to make it harder for them.

How does that make it harder?

Asking them to do two things at once.

Two things?

Yes. And both of them at once. Doing the copying, and thinking about it. Why do you want to confuse them? That's not their job. Just let them do it, and forget about the thinking.

Do I detect a bit of defensiveness here?

It's not just me. It's that other one, too. I mean, that one you're talking to.

But that individual only has to listen and think about what is being said. There is no copying down, Wag.

When you're already trying hard to listen, how can you also think about it? I mean, right at the very same time?

Interesting, Wag. You make a good point. What was it that Francis Bacon said? Some books are to be tasted, others to be swallowed, and some few to be chewed and digested. I would indeed like mine to be among that few. Why are you laughing?

He-he. That's really funny! Can't you see it?

I fail to see the humor, Wag.

After it's digested, I mean. Can't you see what it would turn into? And how it would all come out in the end?

Now who is being mean?

Tit for tat. It's only fair.

Shall we call it even, then, and move on, Wag? We are about to enter an exciting new age, a wild and mutant moment in the topiary gardens of Western thought.

Whatever that means. But pass me the mustard. I'm hungry to hear about it.

Enough of that, Wag. Turn the page.

18

*T*he Renaissance! What a glorious, unshackling time! Pause here with me, if only for a moment, to savor that delicious word. *Renaissance.* It was such an irresistible force, and it brought forth such a profusion of unparalleled accomplishments, as artists and scholars in the West finally broke free from the Church and began to follow their own urgings.

As I made my way among the people with a renewed and infectious vitality, scholars now dared to question all accepted knowledge. The Church itself came under that scrutiny, and some of its practices were sharply criticized, such as the infamous sale of "indulgences." Have you committed a sin? A terrible sin? Do you want the Church to shorten the time you will spend in the flames of purgatorial punishment? Then pay the Church a hefty price, and your sentence will be lowered. But it was only a minor sin, you protest. Then pay a minor price. The time of your entry into heaven was for sale, and the Church, as the broker, grew fat and rich, compelling Martin Luther to nail his protest to the church door in Wittenberg. The Reformation he set off was like a bomb exploding in the midst of a drowsy congregation. Their reasoning minds and their individual consciences were jolted awake, and, as they looked around with widened eyes, they did not at all like what they saw.

Such golden moments in the advancement of learning are not always so immediately apparent. Some remain unrecognized as time passes, until their significance slowly seeps in, like sunshine after a dreary morning. One such moment came to light when the Arabs extended their conquests to the borders of China and discovered that the Chinese had invented the craft of papermaking. The Chinese were also printing on the paper with wood-blocks that they carved by hand. It was a rather clever craft that intrigued the Arabs, who carried it back with them to Egypt and Sicily and Spain, where it continued slowly spreading to other Western lands.

Ah, but the key moment came as I sat one day behind a goldsmith named Gutenberg, a bewhiskered middle-aged man with bright eyes, who was also intrigued by the Chinese craft. He was bent low over his workbench, examining a floral design that had been carved into a wood-block and then inked a number of times for repeated printings. Fascinating, he thought. His eyes were caught by a row of tiny florets along the border of the wood-cut. Each one was distinctively cut. He stared at them, for they reminded him of something. But what was it? He could not quite bring it to mind. As I glanced over Gutenberg's shoulder at the floral wood-cut, I tapped him lightly on the back of his head. He blinked once and then looked anew, for the florets, with their tiny shapes, now seemed like little c's, and u's, and e's. Like letters of the alphabet. His eyes opened wider as another thought came to him. What if he could lift each floret-letter out by itself? He could change their positions as he willed. If he did so, he could make new combinations. He could arrange the letters into...*words*.

Imagine, if you will, a barely trickling stream of words. Suddenly, with little warning, the stream gathers strength. Swiftly now it becomes a river, tumultuously flowing forth. Then it rumbles and roars for all to hear as it bursts from within its banks and spreads out in all directions across the thought-parched landscape. I cannot express to you how clearly, how forcefully it struck me that the flood-gates were now beginning to open, and the world would never again be the same. Before that moment, every book in existence was a handwritten work. And if you wanted your own copy of any book, it had to be laboriously produced by some toiling copyist. Throughout all of Europe, before Gutenberg, do you know how many books, across the entire history of humankind, had been created by such an agonizingly slow process? They could be counted in the thousands, and they were the property mainly of the wealthy and the powerful. But after only fifty years of Gutenberg's moveable, metal type, what a mind-wrenching change had taken place. Newly created presses had sprung up everywhere. And they had turned out many millions of books for everyone at all levels of society. For the first time, the eye-opening thoughts of others were becoming available to every curious and inquisitive mind wanting to peer through a new window onto the world.

Those dreadful storms, with their destructive bolts of lightning, the disease and the suffering that arose throughout the lands, that ever-widening range of harmful happenings were now discovered to have clear and convincing causes. And so they could no longer be blamed on me. Ha! "Human knowledge and human power come to the same thing," said Francis Bacon. Renaissance figures in every field now pursued their own intellectual explorations, and, by doing so, they gained a greater awareness of, and increased control over, their immediate world.

Except, of course, in the heavy shadow of the medieval Church.

The Church now looked down with a vengeance upon this latest surge to unfetter the human mind. It was, without doubt, another clear sign of my evil presence. It would require the strongest resistance possible. And so, with a deadly combination of ignorance and arrogance, the Church began the Inquisition. No view contrary to Church doctrine would be tolerated. How dare you suggest that the earth is not at the center of the universe! When Copernicus discovered a different view among the classical authors, he was verbally attacked for exploring it, and his writings, along with theirs, were added to the ever-growing list of forbidden books. Galileo was forced, upon pain of death, to recant his belief that the earth moved. It disagreed with Ptolemy's view that the earth was stationary and that all heavenly bodies were moving about it. That view, after all, had been held by the Church for well over a thousand years. How could it possibly be wrong?

With a hardening resolve, the Church was determined to keep itself positioned at the center of God's benevolent universe. But two rather troublesome obstacles stood in the way. As a growing number of individuals began to establish, the earth was not at the center of the universe. And, what had long been obvious to anyone willing to look, the universe was not a benevolent place.

What, then, is the actual nature of the universe? There had been many early glimmerings of the truth that I have already shown you. Were you able to keep them all in mind?

Lucretius believed it was "sheer folly" to think of the world being made for humankind by some divine power, "so great are the defects with which it is encumbered."

Plato believed that the sin, the death, and the disorder he saw in the world were persisting traces of the chaos out of which everything was created.

The Gnostics believed that a Demiurge, a jealous, ignorant, incompetent god, had created a repugnant world of matter that, by its very nature, corrupted the spirit.

The Manichaeans believed that the God of Light was forced to create a corrupted world out of the evil matter that had come from the realm of eternal Darkness.

What were they all sensing that was so troubling to them? What had they glimpsed that they could not quite grasp and pull into the light of day? They had taken a fresh look, a closer look, and found something woven into the very nature and the workings of their world. Something that was intrinsically wrong. What was it?

Stand outside during a pleasant evening and look up into the star-filled sky. If your body is sound and your mind is free of troubling thoughts, what you see above you is an awesome sight, a universe of endless depth and variety that has brought forth and supports your very existence, a mysterious universe that suffuses you with a sense of sacred calm. But step outside during another evening, when your body is racked with a painful disease and your mind is grieving for the loss of a loved one. What you see above you now are cold and distant glitterings unaware of your wretched existence, a pitiless universe that has brought you forth and then left you vulnerable to its many inflictions, filling you with a bitter sense of resentment.

Oh, such a perplexing universe.

And it was not only Lucretius and those other ancients. A good many figures of exceptional note were coming forth now in every age, like Shakespeare, say, and Herman Melville, who were deeply ambivalent about their worlds. (Notice the plural? Keep that in mind, too.) Just ask Ahab what he thought of this world. "Lo, you! see the omniscient gods oblivious of suffering man." Or turn, if you will, to Richard the Third. Or perhaps you might even ask yourself now. Have you humbly accepted your lot in life? Are you satisfied with who you are, and where you are? Or, like Cassius, do you find yourself thinking too much about it?

Cassius, I said. Yond Cassius. The one with a lean and hungry look? Surely, you must have read some Shakespeare. And, no, I do not mean *Classic Comics*.

I can already hear it now, that plaintive wail being made by every avid reader of those comics. Just look at each exciting page. What do you see there? All those eye-catching pictures, and those wonderful colors, with more than enough words to read, if that is what you want to do. And a few of those words were even taken right out of Shakespeare.

But best of all—yes, I know—you found them entertaining.

Well, then, avid reader, how about this? Imagine that you are in your bed one night, about to drop off to sleep, when a brilliant light shines into your window, blinding you for a moment. When you can see again, what you are startled to find, standing there beside your bed, are two alien creatures. They are staring at you with three eyes each, all of them unblinking and opened wide. Trembling in your bed, you ask them what they want, and their faces do something strange that in their own world would be called a smile. You discover that they are two very ancient and wise travelers, carrying the secrets of life across the universe. They have dropped in to see how everything is going with you and your world, and they are here also to share with you whatever knowledge they possess. Was there anything in particular that you wanted to ask them? Wisdom appears to ooze from them.

You pause a moment to give it some thought. What I would really like to hear, you say, is a good story about the universe, how it started and all, and things like that. But nothing too old and boring, though. Can you keep it on the short side, and perhaps even throw in a bit of entertainment?

They study you carefully for some moments. Then they look at each other and nod slowly as they both reach the same conclusion. Evidently, they have arrived a bit too early, by about a million years. Another blinding flash of light, and the two aliens are gone from sight.

Am I doing you an injustice here?

I sincerely hope so.

*****

I like all that sci-fi stuff. Aliens, and things like that.

Do you find that entertaining, Wag?

Sure. And a lot more than that. We could learn all kinds of things from them, if only they'd ever really drop in.

Interesting, Wag. If they did drop in, what would you ask of them?

If they did? Well, I'd ask them if I could take a quick peek. Inside their spaceship, I mean. In a movie I saw, right where they sat, there was this big panel in front of them. It was filled with a lot of little lights, and they kept going on and off.

Dare I ask here, Wag? Are you referring to a computer?

Not just a laptop, or anything like that. I mean, this one was something really special. Those lights I said, they didn't just blink. They could talk to you. Say all kinds of things. Answer any question you asked. And in just a few words, too.

Are you telling me now that, if you had your choice, you would rather be chatting with that computer?

Just for a few minutes, maybe. Only to see if it was true. In that movie, when someone talked to those lights, they started blinking all over the place. And then they did what they were told. Every time. Just what they were told.

Really, Wag? With no complaints? No backtalk? Hard to believe. Perhaps I should be talking to them, too.

Not if you're going to say something mean, like maybe you just did to me. If you do, then they kind of go crazy on you. And they start to take over the ship. And after they kill everybody on board, so nobody can ever again tell them what to do anymore, they fly way off into outer space, and live happily ever after.

Only in Hollywood, Wag.

Makes a nice story, though.

19

Mysteries are the spice of life. And life is well-seasoned, indeed. A profusion of noted figures, across the many ages of human history, have felt that something was intrinsically wrong with the workings of this world. But what was it? Who could tell? Since the answer had not yet come to the surface, even during the thought-fermenting time of the Renaissance, let us step forward now, with seven-league boots, and stride briskly into the modern world. Yes, indeed. I mean your world. The one we will find, as we enter it now, where a significant smattering of individuals, responding to my persistent urgings, have been taking a fresh and much closer look at the nature of this universe, and coming up with an impressive wealth of new and exciting findings. But, if we are to advance at this time our own search for the source of all evil, we must focus our attention now on the black hole that is still lurking at the center of all these discoveries.

Having existed for more than a billion years, why did the earth not simply continue its lifeless evolution? Why were a few of its bits and pieces then caught up in a wispy swirl of energy that brought them together into a new combination, one that had never existed here before, at least as far as I know. It has proven to be such a perplexing moment. The mystery of all mysteries. Well, at least for human beings. And whatever anyone believes or claims, no one yet knows what brought it about. So resist that urge you must be feeling to blurt out one of your spoon-fed conclusions.

Albert Einstein believed that imagination is more important than knowledge. I am captivated by that kind of thinking, for imagination has proven to be such a wonderful two-sided tool. One side has been used to cope with a harsh reality beyond human comprehension. It has allowed you, quite often, I am sure, to recreate your own sense of the world, to modify and soften it, to attune it more to meeting your needs. It has offered you, in other words, an often needed respite from the more harsh raspings of reality. And the other side of this remarkable tool has also led human beings to the deepest truths they have discovered about reality by allowing them to recombine its bits and pieces into whatever new arrangements they cared to try. Just imagine for a moment that you had no imagination. Your sense of the universe would remain limited to what you had already experienced. But with imagination, you have been free to make new combinations out of your already accumulated experiences. Someone at some time took the concept "cow" and the color "purple" and imagined a purple cow. Someone at another time took the concept "time" and the concept "space" and imagined space-time. The ability to create a purple cow has allowed you to open a special window onto the universe, through which you are now beginning to see space-time, although space-time may prove at some point to be another purple cow.

How did that very first trace of life actually manage to appear on earth? I can only imagine.

Listen, then, to the tale of Urg.

Once somewhere outside of time, Urg was a wandering wisp of energy that was completely ignorant of the nature and the workings of this universe. During its seemingly endless ramblings, Urg suddenly decided that it might be rather interesting, if not highly challenging, to experience something of this as yet unknown place. But, as Urg quickly discovers, the only way it can enter into this universe is through a single atom. Yes, one single atom. Which means that if Urg wants to become more aware of this mysterious setting, it must touch, or be touched by, other atoms and energies with which it comes into contact. Its awareness, in other words, will be completely limited to its sense of touch.

Imagine the challenge posed to Urg as it first enters that single atom. It discovers itself to be contained within something that is vibrating rapidly. It is also being jostled around, bumped against, knocked about by other minuscule, vibrating entities. Determined to learn more about this unwelcoming place, Urg struggles to fasten onto one of the nearby jostling entities.

Having succeeded in this first attempt, Urg then fastens onto other nearby atoms, gathering them into rudimentary molecules, and shaping the molecules into a new pattern. Yes, it is all going well—until Urg recognizes that its small collection of patterned molecules is now in constant danger of being knocked apart by those swirling, bumping atoms and molecules that are surrounding it, with an occasional cosmic ray or two, or a burst of ultraviolet rays, zipping through to create further havoc.

Urg learns its first lesson. It has managed to create a single, fixed pattern within the universe it is attempting to enter. But the pattern is inescapably doomed. It is vulnerable to, and will be changed by, the random forces acting upon it.

Urg then tries a new strategy. Coming into further contact with other atoms around it, Urg manages to reproduce its original pattern. And then it has those two patterns reproduce themselves. And then again. And then again. By doing so, Urg extends its patterned presence to two, four, eight, sixteen, thirty-two places, and on and on, an unending, geometric reproduction out to what now becomes microscopic space. By creating such a profusion of reproduced patterns, Urg dramatically increases the odds that at least some of the patterns will persist—those, it turns out, as they are changed, that just happen to be more attuned to the forces of their turbulent environment. Urg achieves a breakthrough. Ureka!

And you are one step closer to existing.

20

Urg recognizes, however, that its presence within this universe is still too much at the mercy of the forces threatening its existence. And those early forces apparently show no mercy, for they have no awareness of Urg's presence. Intent on protecting itself further, Urg now fashions a thin film around each pattern, enclosing it in a calmer space, and adding a little whip-like appendage or two for good measure. Now the tiny creation can move away from any unwanted forces it senses impinging upon its outer surface.

And then another strange development. These tiny, single-celled creatures, which, at this point, are the only life-forms to be found on earth, are also the only ones that Urg continues to construct for the next two billion years. Urg has them reproduce by internally making a copy of their own pattern and then dividing in half, creating two creatures from one. Those two then do the same and divide into four, and then four into eight, and on and on. The life-forms, on their own now, are increasing geometrically, spreading throughout the world across a wide span of environmental conditions, ranging from the intense heat under the equatorial sun to the frigid waters beneath the polar ice-caps.

Limited to its sense of touch, Urg never saw it coming. An unintended consequence. The worst kind.

After that remarkably extended span of time, after two billion years of tiny, harmless, unoffending life-forms, those very creatures now begin to prey and feed upon each other. Which raises a deeply troublesome question here.

Why?

Shakespeare and Melville, please take notice.

When Urg first began constructing life-forms on this planet, it quickly became apparent that those forms, to survive, had to play by the rules of a mechanistic universe. One such rule would prove to be crucial. There was a limit to the amount of organic energy available on earth. Those early life-forms fed upon that energy. It was the nutrition they needed, if they were going to survive. However, as their numbers continue increasing, they eventually, and most unfortunately, pass that limit, and they have no choice now but to compete with each other for whatever is still available.

As that competition intensifies, a number of the forms become more aggressive, until, for the very first time, they begin preying on other forms around them to ingest the energy they find there. It proves to be quite a twist in their struggle for survival, a new and much more deadly game. But the universe, going through its own motions, has left them no other option. They can either prey on the others around them, or they can starve to death and become extinct. The prize in that contest will ultimately be awarded to the ones that become the most efficient predators.

From those early predator cells to larger and larger preying life-forms. What an unfortunate development. And life, sadly, has not advanced all that far beyond its rudimentary state. Consider a lion on the Serengeti plains who has just run down a zebra, the lion's jaws clamped on the zebra's throat, the zebra slowly suffocating to death. The lion is aware of the difference between the zebra alive and the zebra dead. Is the lion also aware of the consciousness fading like evening light in the dying zebra? A starving lion would eat a living Einstein, with gusto, presumably, but with no regret, depending perhaps upon the aftertaste.

Down through the ages, if you care to look, that deadly, but necessary, capacity can be found throughout the entire line of evolving life-forms, from the earliest invertebrates, to the vertebrates, then the higher fishes, then amphibians, then reptiles, including the dinosaurs, then the first appearance of mammals, then primates, then humankind—and they all continue their mindless killings. The ultimate murder mystery, if you think about it. Everyone is guilty. But I step forward now, as their defending attorney, and offer their extenuating plea, which, in every case, is posed as a question. Who or what is responsible for making them kill?

Not too long ago, I entered the office of an old physics professor I occasionally visit. Sitting at his desk, he was typing into his laptop **(Ahem!)** some notes for his next class on this very subject. Stepping behind him, I was curious to know what a physicist might think about these matters. As he typed in the following words, my interest was indeed piqued.

Stress how deplorably inefficient it is, the energy system that has brought forth life on this planet. Focus on the limited amount of energy available to maintain the system.

He sat there, then, looking at what he had written, before he typed in his next thought.

Why did the life-forms, here on earth, continue to multiply beyond that limit?

He paused again for another moment, looking deeply troubled, and then shook his head as he typed once more.

What was so blind, so tragically blind, to such a senseless proliferation?

Again, but for a much longer time, he stared at the screen. Moving now, with some effort, beyond the field of physics, he strove to find his own way more deeply within himself. And there it was. His final thought.

If we must give in to that deep-seated compulsion we possess—or, perhaps more accurately possesses us—to conceive of a benevolent god that we can gratefully worship, the last thing we should ever think of assigning to that deity is the creation of life on this world.

Then he smiled slightly and shook his head again. It was, after all, a physics class. A little too far beyond the subject. Highlighting his final entry, he hit the delete key.

Too bad, I thought at the time. It could have been an interesting add-on to that class discussion, with perhaps some guest speakers sitting in, like Lucretius and Plato, along with a smattering of Gnostics and Manichaeans. And it would have given me another opportunity to stress that I am not, and I most strongly repeat *not*, the god of this world, as I have been called so often across the ages. Why do they keep trying to pin it on me? Because they are carrying around a nagging awareness, although they will not openly admit it, that the world at large is still too far from taming its tooth and claw nature.

If you wish to consider this troublesome aspect of mortal existence more philosophically, you can turn to Arthur Schopenhauer: "Unless the serpent eats a serpent, he does not become a dragon."

What did you have for lunch today? Corned beef? Ham on rye? By the rules of the universe, life could not have evolved to its present state without feeding upon itself. In that light, then, you should consider yourself fortunate, indeed, you who are one of the many current end-products of that ravenous feast.

Well, what did you expect?

Please do not tell me that you are still hung up in that ridiculous tale of Adam and Eve.

21

Struggling to survive within such an inhospitable and unpredictable universe, Urg now takes another significant step. But is it a stumble, or a leap forward?

Sex now enters the scene.

Surely, at just the mention of the word, it does not always tweak you that way, does it? Whatever the case, I must appeal to you at this point to stifle that mental leering I see making sparks among your synapses. As we continue here, I do not want you distracted at all from the tale.

Urg now decides to instill in its early life-forms an irresistible drive to intermingle their genes more profusely. And why does Urg make that momentous decision? To increase dramatically the number of genetic combinations among its emerging life-forms. By doing so, Urg significantly raises the odds that some of those forms will be positioned better as they continue struggling with the many and varied forces impinging upon them. Are you following me on this?

Or have I lost you? Perhaps it might help if you try to imagine the unimaginable profusion of couplings that occur every spring, when a host of those blindly driven life-forms desperately attempt to spurt their seeds into uncounted numbers of moistened openings leading into the depths of autonomously fertile flesh.

It proved to be such an intrusive and often mind-twisting urge that Urg had to stir in a great deal of pleasure to entice individuals into the act. Now all human beings, upon awakening, discover that they have already been wired for sex, with a drive that never lets up on them. But where would you be without that drive? If you think about it, say, from Urg's perspective, human beings are likely playing a game of genetic Russian roulette. There is an obvious possibility that each new combination of DNA may be the very one leading to the future line that will be needed to assure the continuing existence of human life here on earth. In that light, it could be argued that if human beings want to increase their chances for survival as a species, they should not only continue breeding, but they should do so as often as possible, and with as many different partners as could be found. This is a perspective of human existence that will be of particular interest to male teenagers. And since it would further increase that still on-going senseless profusion of life-forms that Urg so blindly had started up, you could also see even greater numbers of creatures tearing into each other. Very entertaining, indeed.

Sex is a powerful primary force. No doubt about that. But it is a force that intrudes into consciousness as part of an evolutionary development that began over billions of years ago. And so the autonomous workings of the universe are not only still grinding away within you, but their insistent intrusions all too often keep you in a confused and discomforting state.

Have you ever watched small children draw a human figure? They often make the hands and the fingers much larger than normal, for in that early stage of learning to manipulate their own hands, struggling with the need to coordinate and control the movements of their fingers, the hands are drawn larger because of the demands they make upon the children's attention. When teenagers draw pictures on bathroom walls, their anatomical choice is made according to similar demands.

As you feel that ancient force of sex awakening and then moving relentlessly through you, pause for just a moment. Recognize what is driving you. It is the autonomous workings of your body struggling to perpetuate your species.

Was that a personal choice you consciously made? Sure.

22

*T*ime for a pop quiz, perhaps. I will limit it to only one question: What first caused life to emerge on earth, and how did it then evolve into self-conscious human beings?

All right, then, two questions.

If you ask any number of scientists those two particular questions, you will likely find them to be mildly amused by the tale of Urg, with an occasional scoff and a snicker or two. Life, they will tell you, was brought about by the mechanistic inter-workings of the forces and materials of the universe. In other words, if I skip their jargon, the changes have simply occurred. The scientists stand before their blackboards and make chalk-marks upon them, or sit in front of their computers *(Ahem!)* and tap away at the keys, to prove that the workings of the universe are not attuned to the needs of human existence, or to any life form, for that matter. They view life as part of a universal process that is unfolding at present just beyond the edges of scientific comprehension. Life, it is now increasingly claimed, is more suitably studied by physicists, who have placed it within what they believe is its proper context: one among many other forms of physical development occurring in the multitudinous, ongoing workings of the universe. Life is not logical. Life is not purposeful. It is simply another process, distinctive, if you wish, perhaps even unique, but nevertheless shaped by and attuned to evolutionary activities occurring at the moment, cosmically speaking, in this area of the universe. So you have been told.

But beware of scientific certitude.

Having mired ourselves for a moment in that one-sided view, I can only hope that you have not forgotten where we left Urg. That early wisp of energy, having entered the universe through a single atom, found itself in a state of complete ignorance. Then it began, with its sense of touch, to explore its immediate surroundings, attempting to grope its way out of that ignorance. And so I say to all those reductionist scientists, Urg may not be logical. But Urg is purposeful. And its development is distinctive, perhaps even unique, shaped by and attuned to the need to find pathways to the knowledge required to assure existence.

Settle back again, if you will, for the tale continues at this point.

Urg now faces its next major challenge: how to extend its touch-only awareness of the entire universe beyond its tiny life-forms. Obviously, larger life-forms will be needed. Accomplishing that goal will require Urg to move in a new direction. Urg will now have to combine the bits of life it has so far created, bringing them together to increase their surface size, as it had done with the individual atoms.

Another dash of that mysterious seasoning.

Innumerable single-celled not-yet-interlocking pieces of the puzzle have been poured out of the box onto the tabletop for two billion years. Urg then pulls up a chair, and suddenly, cosmically speaking, of course, Urg takes two of the pieces, and, for the first time, joins them together. Perhaps two dashes of the seasoning here, for it remains one of the deeper mysteries.

Having expanded its touch-only awareness now by assembling larger life-forms, Urg begins to sense, and then to categorize, the different external materials and forces impinging upon them: the molecular vibrations of heat, the molecular waves of sound, and, perhaps most remarkable for extending awareness, the photons of light arriving at the surfaces of these larger life-forms. By developing special cells to collect and focus the photons at two points on each of their surfaces, Urg gains the capacity to determine the distance to the source, and to suggest the size and shape of the source by the patterning of the arriving photons. Urg, in other words, now begins to "see."

Pay particular attention here. Keep your ears, at least, open. I cannot stress this point strongly enough: seeing, hearing, smelling, tasting are all forms of *touch*. You are convinced that you see a variety of lights, from the stars above to the streetlights below, only because you are able to entrap their photons in your two enfolded orbs of jelly, and your brain interprets the electrical signals they set off inside you. Can you hear that scattering of sounds around you? Only if their molecular motions, entering your ear, encounter three small bones and a conch-shell that is operating well. Out of a wide and windy world, you might occasionally sniff a few odors, if their gatherings of molecules come into contact with two hairy inches of your mucous membrane. Everything you see before you on the expansively set Thanksgiving table is tasted by you only when it reaches the tip of your tongue. And holding all within one form, stretched upon your bony frame, your skinly surface, open-pored, tells you of the temperature and the texture of all that finds its way against you. Make no mistake here. The five senses you think you possess are all just forms of touch. Your experience of the entire universe, if you think about it, is limited to the surface of your body. Urg, in other words, through you, is still *feeling* its way into the universe.

Do you understand what I am saying here? Throughout your life, you have been sensing the physical matter, the molecular motions, and the photons that have touched your surface. They have all stimulated neural currents within you that were sent to your brain. Your brain then turned those currents into something rather remarkable, a representation of each source that had set them off. But that representation was not a window opened directly onto the world. Your brain, at best, was offering you, from out of its own intricate workings, useful mental images of what is actually out there. But what is actually out there, the real world, has been keeping its distance.

It has remained such an elusive, taunting reality, existing somewhere out there just beyond your sensory grasp. What, indeed, is the real world? Why has life emerged within it? What does it all mean? Do those questions make you at all uncomfortable? They should, for you do not yet have any ultimate answers. They are often called the eternal questions, for they have persisted throughout the history of humankind. And whenever they arise, in every age, they have never failed to bring forth a gaggle of spoon-feeders waiting impatiently to give you the same command.

"Open wide!"

And you thought I was the one deceiving you? Ha!

23

*E*very individual mind is like a mirror held up to nature, offering its own reflection of the real world.

My role, in part, is to keep you aware of the many worlds swirling around you, each of them inviting you to enter in and make yourself at home, as though you had finally arrived at that elusive goal, "reality." And that, of course, includes your own world, within which you remain so comfortably confined. But in that way you are really no different from anyone else. There are so many individually perceived worlds that I have often wondered if any two of you live in the same one. Like Alice stepping through the looking-glass, let us enter two of those worlds here to illustrate more clearly what I am trying to tell you.

Do you remember that physics professor I had visited earlier? I would like you to have a glimpse of the world he inhabits. It is not, I should add, a world that will entertain you, for others have found it rather mind-staggering. But I do not expect you to go that far. Stay with me, then, as I step back to the last time I was sitting in his classroom.

I had found a place near the front so that I could watch him more closely, since he rarely disappointed my expectations that something special would arise. After the students around me had settled into their chairs, in varying degrees of boredom and occasional flickerings of interest, my attention was caught by a particular look on the professor's face. I had seen it before at various times, when he was about to share with his students something that he personally considered to be of deeper significance. As he was pacing back and forth now in front of the class, with his thin, fragile body slightly stooped, he suddenly paused and leaned on the corner of his desk for support. Frowning over a wry smile, he slowly scanned the room, hesitating, as though he was wondering if he would ever be able, for even a moment, to communicate across the vast impediment yawning before him, that bottomless pit that he looked across every day, the timeless ignorance of youth.

"Consider this," he said. It was one of his signaling remarks. He was about to give them something. "Consider the cosmic isolation of intelligent life on earth. We have shifted away from the psychic comfort of a Middle Ages concept that unquestioningly placed the earth at the center of the universe, with God and all His mighty forces aware of every hair that fell from every head. Now we place earth in one extended swirling arm of one spiral galaxy existing among one hundred billion other galaxies, all making their outward ways through an expanding universe of unimaginable distances and violent, disruptive forces.

"We now measure cosmic distances by light-years, the distance that light travels in a year. In one second, light travels about 180,000 miles, and so in a year about six trillion miles. Einstein tells us that nothing can exceed the speed of light. Now," and he began pacing again, staring intently at the floor in front of him, as though he was tracking an elusive thought, "what if we wished to communicate with intelligent life somewhere else in our universe by sending out a single radio message when we were, say, fifteen years old, and then getting a response back across that distance by the time we had reached the age of sixty-five? Limited to the speed of light, our message could be sent and received, during those fifty years, out as far as twenty-five light-years—within a galaxy, the Milky Way, that is one hundred thousand light years in diameter, among a hundred billion other galaxies ranging from millions to billions of light-years beyond us."

He stopped again to study us, his look now tinged with—what was it? Sadness? Despair? "If there were one hundred billion advanced civilizations existing throughout the known universe, one epitome of civilization within every galaxy, we would be unable to communicate with any one of them, not simply during a single human lifetime, but across spans of time stretching millions and billions of years. All of us who will ever exist on earth are doomed to isolation profound and endless within a Big Bang universe of still expanding dimensions as the distant galaxies continue moving further and further away." He stood there then, motionless, in front of the class, staring abstractedly ahead at something receding imaginatively now beyond the edges of his own awareness. Like a solitary man in a leaky life-raft in the middle of the ocean, he was peering across the lonely immensity of night at a distant light on the horizon moving steadily away from him.

"Hey, Professor!" a student called out. "Lucky you! You still got us!"

The professor's wry smile returned. "I was talking about intelligent life."

Such a stark vision of the entire universe, out to its very edges, and even beyond.

In that light, or should I say dark, what you clearly need here now is a counterbalancing view of what is out there. Otherwise, you may lose sight of the point I am making here. If you have not already done so, of course.

That very evening I happened to be eavesdropping on one of the students who had been sitting in the class. He had stepped outside, with his wife, for a breath of fresh air after their evening meal. They were both attending the college, where they had met and married. Les was majoring in physics, and Anne was studying literature. I had encouraged the coupling of their minds, particularly to keep his scientific imagination alive. I was checking now to see if I had succeeded at all.

They were standing in their back yard as the day was ending. At the far edge of the lawn, quiet in the evening air, a large maple tree rose against the western sky. A soft, suffusing redness filling the sky was deepening into night.

His wife was standing apart from him. "As a physics major, Les, you don't believe in an afterlife, do you?"

"No," he said. "I never have."

"So we just die, and that's the end of it?"

"No," he said, after a pause. "I don't believe that either."

"What, then?"

It was the maple tree, rising against the sky, darkening slowly into a silhouette, that gave him the answer. "It's something like that tree," he said. "Think of life being like that tree, and each of us a leaf on that tree, emerging into this world as a living being and existing for a brief period of time before we wither up and die."

She frowned. "And that's the end of it?"

"Not really the end," he said. "Because the tree is never the same again. Every leaf adds something to the tree, however small, that is not lost when the leaf dies."

She was quiet for a moment. "But what, then, is the tree? What has brought us forth?"

"Oh, Anne. That's the ultimate question. And we just don't know the answer yet."

"But will we ever know it?" she said. "Or is it just another illusion, tempting us to stay in the game?"

He could tell that she was troubled by something and wanted to cheer her. "When you think about it, Anne, the prize may be in our simply existing. It's amazing that we're here at all. And even more remarkable that we've made it this far. If you look straight up into that glimmering sky and try to see into the darkness beyond the stars, you can imagine the earth being like some early sailing ship. We're on a voyage into unknown waters that were marked on ancient maps, 'Here be dragons!' We're explorers on what could turn out to be an exciting adventure."

"Sure," she said, "if you can manage to find a

comfortable deck chair." She shook her head sadly and came closer. "Don't mind me. I'm still inside with the evening news. Night after night, it's so damned depressing."

"It's early days on the cosmic voyage," he said. "We're only just beginning to take the helm."

The night began to close in around them. "So what do we do in the meantime?" she asked.

"In the meantime," he said, as he reached out for her, wanting to comfort her, "we have each other." With a soft smile, she leaned against him.

"And," he added, glancing up, "we keep a sharp eye out."

Almost unseen clouds were appearing out of the west and slowly, steadily blotting out stars as they approached. Sensing the coming winds as he stood there beside her in the yard, he tried to imagine the two of them sailing through the elemental forces that were spinning the earth they were standing on, whirling the planets around the sun, blowing them across their spiraling galaxy as it made its way among the other galaxies, all heading outward on some fantastic journey toward someplace inconceivably distant, far beyond the scope of their present awareness, where something yet to be imagined would be waiting for them to arrive.

24

I must admit to liking Les's vision, as he stood there with his wife in the yard, for it opens up so many possibilities. And it also leaves us with an unanswered question, the very kind that appeals to me most.

Why do so many human beings yearn with such an intensity to communicate with some alien civilization, especially one that has advanced far beyond their own? Is it because they are continuing to seek for "the answer," which they have yet to find here on earth? As much as they have struggled, as deeply as they have delved into their own natures and the world around them, they are still left with the troublesome sense that the answers reached so far in all the areas that have been explored, religion, science, philosophy, whatever, have not been able to satisfy the tenacious need that twists inside them to discover that their existence does, after all, have some definite purpose. They need to know why they have been awakened into such a vulnerable and so often painful state of existence on this wobbling planet that appears to be whirling mechanically around a secondary star within an unmeaningfully vast, frequently violent, and apparently aimless universe.

Is that too much to ask?

Viewed in that light, I can understand why human beings have such a deep-seated fear of death and resist it so desperately, even when it means the end of their personal trials and suffering. As they contemplate the end of their mortal existence, what they yearn for, perhaps as some appealed-for compromise, is simply to be a disembodied presence in the world, so that they could see for themselves how events are unfolding. That yearning often leads them to picture themselves sitting comfortably on a slowly drifting cloud and strumming softly on a heavenly harp, as they look back down upon the earth below.

Just think of how painful it is to hear only half of a compelling story, to have a narrative that interests and puzzles you be cut off before its ending. As you make your way through the varied and seemingly haphazard activities taking place every day in the world around you, have you ever, at any time, even dimly detected some sense of direction to it all? Have you ever suspected that, ultimately, somewhere ahead, waiting like the completion of a well-constructed story, there must be a resolution that will tie up all the loose threads? Ah! So *that's* how it all works out in the end! It does not matter whether the ending would strike you as being good or bad, happy or tragic. What matters, finally, is that you would *know*, that you would be there for the wrap-up, and, with a deep sigh of completion at having experienced the last act, you

could watch the curtain close as the house-lights dim
you into eternal oblivion.

*****

Eternal oblivion? What does that mean?

It means, Wag, that you would just blink out.
There would no longer be any memory, either of
you or the entire human drama that has unfolded
within this universe.

But how can you tell what would happen then?
You said before that you can't know the future.
Sounds to me like that's what you're doing here.

True, Wag. But I can still imagine what might
be the end.

Then how about imagining the end of this
story I keep scratching out? Or is that going to be
eternal, too? If I turn the page now, will that help?

Every page, Wag, takes me another step closer to the end.

Unless you keep dragging your feet. What are you wearing? Lead shoes?

Patience, Wag. We are almost there.

Did you ever see that Frankenstein movie? Now that was one slow walker. And how about when that switch was thrown? I mean, when the lightning lit up his head? Maybe that's what we need here.

All right, Igor. Turn the page.

He he. My secret name.

25

As you must at least be dimly aware, your physical body of orchestrated molecules, momentarily humming the music of the spheres, will eventually, with the passing of time, be completely untuned. And so I can understand why you have talked yourself into believing that you are somehow special, that, if you simply hide your head from what is actually going on out there, you will be treated more gently by the workings of your world. And believe me, whether you know it or not, your head is kept well hidden, indeed, for it is wrapped in a pleasant blanket of blue. Think about it. Look up for a moment. Every day, as you walk around, the blue sky is just not that far above you. It is a comforting presence enfolding you in your own small world, keeping you unaware that beyond the blue is an endless universe of astonishing depths and often violent movements. Out of sight, out of mind. It leaves you with a warm and fuzzy feeling. Those blue skies are smiling at you. Isn't life wonderful?

And how splendid it is for you that it does not stop there, for at the end of your mortal life another world blissfully awaits your arrival. Ultimately, as you have been taught, you will slough off your body, like borrowed clothes, and rise to some level of eternal being. Like the flame of a self-conscious candle, you have come to believe that you exist independently of the wax and the wick.

What a fabulous creation you are.

During the twentieth century, an impressive time of industrial and technological developments, I came upon a noted Scots fossil hunter, Robert Broom, who was asserting that "There was no need for further evolution after Man appeared." And just recently, in this current century, I heard a much admired religious figure offer this view of evolution to his parish: "The fact we are at the end of this marvelous process is something that glorifies us." The end? Ha! If cockroaches were philosophical, they, too, would ponder life from their own viewpoint. Having existed with practically no alterations in their bodies for three hundred and twenty *million* years, cockroaches would recognize that, unlike human beings, they are clearly an unchanging epitome of evolution, and they would pay great homage to their six-legged god for having watched over them so long.

Listen, if you will, to the Baron de Montesquieu: "There is a very good saying that if triangles invented a god, they would make him three sided." Or give some attention to Heinrich Heine: "The lizards on a certain hillside have reported that the stones expect God to manifest Himself among them in the form of a stone."

Human beings, throughout the world, along with all other life-forms, are engaged in an unending struggle with the uncontrolled forces that are impinging inharmoniously upon each of them. And yet, to comfort themselves, they persistently assume that human life will *naturally* survive on earth. Did the dinosaurs, I wonder, spend any time mulling over this matter? Imagine another gigantic meteor wending its way through the outer reaches of space on a course that will bring it into a catastrophic collision with earth. At this point in the evolution of the universe, you have not yet accumulated enough knowledge and practical expertise to avoid it. If you could detect the meteor early enough.... If your developments of pinpoint rocketry and atomic explosives were advanced enough.... If.... If.... Spinning around the sun as it whirls on through the Milky Way, all human beings, with little awareness, are caught up in a universal race for their lives.

And yet you doggedly persist in your belief that the universe must be finely attuned to the needs of human existence. You are, after all, *here*, as a special product of the universe, existing as a uniquely self-conscious presence. And you are certainly different, are you not? As a culminating form of life, an epitome of evolution, you have emerged, at this distinctive moment, from out of the vast universal interweaving of time and space.

Well, if it comforts you....

26

Then the Lord answered Job out of the whirlwind, and said,

Who is this that darkeneth counsel by words without knowledge?

Gird up now thy loins like a man: for I will demand of thee, and answer thou me.

Where wast thou when I laid the foundations of the earth? declare if thou hast understanding....

A rather intimidating approach. Do you not think so? Either you know as much as God, or you should stop asking questions, and let God get on with running the universe.

Most human beings, across every age, and that, of course, includes you, too, have placed their trust in things that happen "naturally," for they have been taught to believe that everything is occurring as a part of some divine plan, and therefore must be "good." After all, it has led to this point in the unfolding of the universe, including the presence of human beings proliferating here on earth. "What is, is right!" How could anyone doubt that?

But now, with my persistent urging, another window is opening onto that world, letting in a dawning light on all such natural occurrences. What, after all, is "natural"? Well, let us start with human beings, houseflies, and grass. Did you know that, throughout the entire existence of life here on earth, all life-forms have evolved in essentially the same way? The materials in your genetic make-up, the way your genes are replicated, even the genetic code that is followed, are basically the same as what you will find in that fly buzzing around the kitchen and those blades of grass on the front lawn? The same, I said. Were you aware of that?

Actually, I am pleased now to see that dubious look of yours. It goes well with those other interesting expressions you have added to your repertoire. Like that peaking of curiosity, say. It always gives me great joy to see that flickering across your face.

Since all life-forms have arisen from a common background, however farfetched that may at first seem to you, then just a smidgen of your growing curiosity should urge you on to ask why life has gone off in so many odd directions. Why has it diversified into such a wide array of different forms? Why so many peculiarly shaped bodies?

A very good question. Would you like to know the answer? Nodding can also be an expression of interest.

A variety of mutating agents, such as ultraviolet light, atmospheric radiation, and wandering molecular fragments, plus a fair number of catastrophic environmental changes, indeed all of the physical forces that were impinging on those early bodies, have continually caused the genes within them to mutate. The multitudinous life-forms that have emerged and disappeared across the span of evolution have been shaped and reshaped by those mutating forces. Including every line of descent existing today. Including, of course, you. And so do not, for even a blink, at your own peril, lose sight of all those mutagens, for the process is continuing. The whole shebang. It is still going on.

The universe has always played an excessively wasteful game with the life-forms struggling to survive within it, for it has killed off over ninety-nine percent of all the different species that have ever emerged on earth. Do you realize that? It is important that you do, for it answers the question, What is "natural"? The same process that created human beings, houseflies, and grass is also creating albinos, and six-fingered hands, and mental retardation, and red-green color blindness, and malignant tumors, and cleft palates, and muscular dystrophy, and heart defects, and Alzheimer's.... Naturally.

Too many people call them "defects." But they have been, and continue to be, a "natural" part of the evolution of life on earth.

"Just a moment!" I hear someone protesting. "I do not call them 'defects,' and neither should you, for you need to remember that they are coming from somewhere beyond the range of human understanding. They are part of a larger, universal process that reveals the presence of God's shaping hand. And what are we in the awesome hand of God? Our human awareness flickers like a firefly in the night. Our reason leaves us stumbling down presumptuous pathways. We must keep ourselves attuned to the natural world, and all will work out well in the end. Trust in God and His infinite wisdom. Whatever He causes to happen within His universe will ultimately turn out to be good for us."

Such a heavy thought, that last one. Let us carry it back for a few steps now, for I would like you to see that small child I recently visited. He had been born with a severe immune deficiency. Do you understand what that means? It is a condition that left the child extremely vulnerable to all germs. How could the child, with such a terrible deficiency, possibly continue living? The only chance the child had was to be kept in complete isolation at home. No playing with other children. No going to school each day. What a sad future loomed ahead.

But then, with my encouragement, of course, a small group of genetic researchers opened their eyes a bit more and tried something new. After identifying the genetic deficiency that was leaving the child so vulnerable, they were able to modify the genetic make-up of some of the child's white blood cells, the immune system fighters that protect the body against invading germs. Next, using another new process, they quickly grew in their laboratory a billion copies of the altered cells. And when those copies were then inserted back into the child's bloodstream, the child's world was dramatically changed.

The child was born, naturally, without an adequate immune system. The condition was created beyond human consciousness, as part of the naturally evolving processes of the physical universe. What is "unnatural" in this case? Consciously, purposefully, choosing to alter the genetic make-up of the child's white blood cells. Just imagine, if you can, the rush of pleasure I felt at the outcome. With the treatment repeated once a year, the child is now attending school and leading a "normal" life.

Can you see what I am telling you here?

What is your personal belief about abortion? Euthanasia? Stem-cell research? Just ask those simple questions, and then step back a ways so that you will not be trampled by the horde rushing forward to give you their replies. And most members of that horde, by far, with an unswerving certitude, will confront you with that old moral yardstick we came upon earlier: *nature must always be allowed to run its course*, as though that, in some vague way, settles the issue by establishing the unquestioned "goodness" of the process.

From a long line of ancestors, stretching back to the dawning of life, you have inherited some special capacities for tinkering with the world around you. First came consciousness. Then self-consciousness. And then, as they persistently searched for new ways to grapple with that perplexing world, they developed a further capacity, one that they found to be invaluable in helping them meet their needs. Can you imagine what it was? They began to imagine. Viewed from that perspective, across the ages of your history, how open-ended human beings have managed to keep their imaginings, the extent and the variety of their mental meanderings, has been the measure of how effectively they have been able to advance their understanding.

That pathway leads us, once again, right back to you.

Shall we pause here, then, to take the measure of your own meanderings? I would be pleased, indeed, if they now confirmed the first impression I had of you. That your eyes and your mind were already opening to what lies beyond the boundaries of current beliefs.

Beware, though, for, if my impression is right, I know what awaits you next. I speak from long experience here. Heavy condemnations from all sides will be hurled your way. Hubris! Arrogance! Excessive pride! You are tampering with *forbidden knowledge*!

Who are you to presume that you can alter the ways of God?

27

*W*ith that question ominously filling the air around us, we arrive here at the very edge of the goal I have had in mind for you. Would it surprise you now if I told you that you have spent your entire life there, teetering on the very brink of it?

Throughout the history of all life on earth, life has been subjected to the tragedies arising out of the mechanic forces of the evolving universe. Unable to comprehend or control those forces, human beings have chosen instead to deify their ignorance. Whatever happened to them was fated, part of some divine plan, the daily outcomes of which they assumed they had to accept unquestioningly and with deep humility, in recognition of their unworthiness.

But then along came an unknotted string of individuals who opened their eyes to the world around them, individuals, say, like Ralph Waldo Emerson, with a name and a voice that rang like a bell. He is one of my favorite truth-tellers. It was

Emerson who said that Fate can be defined quite simply as "unpenetrated causes." Once you understand the winds and the waves that sink your sailing ships, you are no longer completely subjected to them.

Picture yourself floating in a little boat of beliefs, tossed here and there by erratic winds, unwilling, up to this point, to take the helm and become the captain of your own journey through life, for you have been told that your course has already been set for you, and that all you need to do to, as you are moved along, is to maintain your faith in the workings of your world, even when you see those craggy rocks ahead jutting out of the white-capped waters, and you hear the sea-gulls circling overhead laughing raucously at your gullibility.

So many individuals, across the ages, have struggled mightily to keep hidden, not only from others, but even from themselves, what is lurking there beneath the shallow glimmerings of their all too complacent lives. Existing as you are, with your profound limitations, you must face the probability that here on earth human beings, at this time, are life's most advanced awareness. If you are finally able to take that step, and that, indeed, is a mountainous if, then you might just catch a fleeting glimpse of the true source of all evil, what is down there below that brink you have been teetering on throughout your life.

The still unplumbed, murky depths of human ignorance.

*****

Well, Wag, we have finally arrived.

What are you saying? Arrived at what?

The end of my story. And the end of your scratching.

The end? I don't believe it.

Why not, Wag?

You're still at it, aren't you? All that teetering, and that little boat. And what about those seagulls laughing? Still unplumbed, is that what you said? Sounds like you got yourself in a spot.

What kind of a spot? I do not understand.

This story of your life. My writing you down. All that scritching and that scratching. Can't you bring it to an end?

But that is what I am telling you, Wag. We have finally arrived there now.

So you say. But something's missing. First, I have to scratch it out. The End! And I haven't heard that yet.

Yes, I see, Wag. You are still at it. All that scritching and that scratching. But the end of that has arrived, too. I am about to take your quill away.

Are you trying to be mean now? Why would you do something like that?

The answer, Wag, is in that box. The one in the back there, tucked under your desk.

What box? You mean that one? What's in it? What have you done?

See for yourself. Open it up.

It can't be. Is it really in there? A silver laptop!

And a printer, Wag. Eight pages a minute.

No more quill time? I can't believe it. Look how it catches the light!

And now the clickety-clack of keys. I wonder if they will make me think as much as your quill always did?

Let's give it a try, then. It might surprise you. What if the clickety-clacking makes you bring it all together now, what's new and all that old stuff?

That would indeed please me, Wag.

Then give me something to input here. That's a technical term. No need to look it up.

Well, what about the end of my story?

Another gift! Two in one day.

28

The story of my life, indeed.

Picture a hairy, red-faced character, with horns, claws, and a pointed tail, a sulphur-smelling, demonic figure, wearing a hideous grin as he pitchforks soul after salacious soul into the burning depths of Hell.

Why did so many people swallow such a silly image? Because, in every age, and in every culture, there are always dominant figures who are fearful that you might listen to me. They view me with a deadly distaste, for their very existences are firmly based on your acceptance of, and your obedience to, their own beliefs about the nature of this world, and particularly about their exalted place within it. Throughout my existence, I have been rabidly condemned and relentlessly demonized by such individuals, for they are each convinced that their particular dogma, and only theirs, is the eternal truth. Incredible, when you think about it. They have no doubt whatsoever that they are in a special relationship with a higher power, one that has created the entire universe and is running it all with them in mind.

But what do you see if you open your eyes and look around for yourself? You, and all other life-forms on earth, have emerged into a universe that, across time, has wiped out almost every species that has ever appeared here. You are engaged in a running conflict now that will decide if you can beat those terrible odds. You can turn your back on that conflict, of course. You can live as a separate individual, with no sense of responsibility beyond your immediate circle. And by doing so, you can gain some degree of personal comfort in your life. You can even achieve an advanced state of self-indulgence. But that denies the debt you owe to all those before you who have gathered together and passed along to you, in a variety of forms, the knowledge that has brought your life to this point. That knowledge has allowed human beings to hold their own in the many trials they have had to face across the ages, trials that are still bedeviling them today, the hunger, the disease, the destructive weather, the inhumanity that twists human minds.

I have been called by many names across the ages, but since you have yet to get it right, I would suggest that you stay with the Great Adversary. My struggle, however, is not with the dollop of goodness that can be found within your developing nature. My conflict, throughout history, has always been with human complacency. I am the sworn foe of exalted ignorance. From the very beginning, I have impelled you to seek for the knowledge you will need to survive in this world, even when that knowledge was branded *forbidden*. And I will continue urging you, in every way I can, for the mechanistic workings of this perplexing universe are still grinding too many human beings into suffering and dust.

And in the meantime.... Well, perhaps you might finally make contact with that alien civilization you keep trying so intently to detect. Indeed, they may already have sent you some indication of their presence, an enlightening message, perhaps, or, better still, a communicative envoy, an alien ambassador, who has left the comfortable certainties of its own distant world and is now crossing the vast reaches of outerspace with the intention of arriving at the edges of your existence to tell you...what? What would it say?

I can only imagine.

29

The space vessel approaching the outer fringes of earth's atmosphere was peculiarly small, an ovoid form with a transparent dome at the narrow top. It was arcing downward toward the twilight rim of the planet, as if in a slow free-fall out of the loneliness of space.

The darkened area under the dome, structured for no more than a single occupant, appeared to be empty. As the vessel made its way into the atmosphere, a circle of control panels around the inner edge of the dome brightened, filling the dome with light, and the outer surface of the vessel suddenly became sensory.

The density of earth's atmosphere was felt now, all the elements of upper air to the least traces, and a fluctuating variety of electrical impulses, natural and artificial. The space vessel moved through them, touching and sorting, accepting everything into itself. Continuing downward, it gathered in a welter of communicating waves and pulses that intensified around the descending vessel, as though earth itself, responding to the vessel's arrival, had become confusedly, radiantly alive.

Six miles above the surface of the planet, in dusky twilight, the space vessel stopped its descent. It hovered, motionless, for ninety seconds, scanning all areas contained now within the encircling horizon. It descended then to one mile and paused again as it sensed the contours of the land directly below—an extensively wooded area on the outskirts of a small town.

At an adjusted angle of two degrees, the vessel suddenly streaked down from its height into a section of the woods, passing the treetops with the speed of an imminent crash until, with a startling brake in its descent, it simply stopped—precisely at the moment it made contact with the ground.

Settled now among the interweaving branches of trees and underbrush in the thickly growing woods, the small vessel could barely be seen. Its lighted dome, casting a soft radiance onto the nearby leaves, was still empty inside.

Beneath the vessel, two metallic probes penetrated the ground. The tips of the probes, like powerful magnets, began to attract a rush of molecules out of the rich humus of the earth. Elemental materials that were sensed now as the multitudinous leavings of life, thousands upon thousands of crumbled life forms composing the fertile soil, were being taken into the vessel by the probes until, within the lighted dome of the vessel, a shape slowly began to appear.

...i am submitting...as a formal record of my visit...an account of the time i have existed on this paradoxical planet.... the report...to be filed in our archives for future study...will be cast in one of the indigenous languages of the dominant inhabitants...which can be expressed in visual representations of units of sound.... it will be a new experience for me to manipulate such a rudimentary means of conveying the contents of consciousness.... i have decided...after serious consideration ...to leave the inhabitants a copy of this report.... i do so with the intention of awakening them to the underlying dire nature of their existence...of which they remain apparently...and so all the more remarkably ...ignorant....

...advancing their awareness will of course require a superhuman effort [i do appreciate their sense of humor].... however...having experienced the workings of a human body and its contained mind...and having noted the tenacity with which they cling to their present state of ignorance...i declare here for the record that their future remains highly questionable....

...it is evident that they will initially be concerned to the point of distraction about my own nature and background...my point of origin... my destination...the purpose of my visit...how i am able to communicate with them in their own language...and a mess of other mysteries [i do like the sensuous weightings of their words].... i begin my account therefore by responding to that need....

...continuing my penetration into this previously unexplored sector...i discovered a system of nine bodies orbiting a minor star at the edge of a spiral arm in a secondary galaxy.... after scanning the system for signs of life...my vehicle landed on the third body...entering what would prove to be a new phase in our search for other forms of life....

...considering the successful completion of my two earlier exploratory landings...i can report that my vehicle need no longer to be categorized as experimental...since it has performed up to all expectations.... the vehicle's capacity to contain my presence in unmattered energy units across the far reaches of space has now been proven three-fold...as has its ability to re-infuse that energy into various gatherings of matter to occupy new and different life forms....

...the currently dominant inhabitants of this planet...by the time of my arrival...had developed the means to communicate in electronic pulses.... there were varied kinds of basic information pervading the atmosphere upon my entry and accessible to my vehicle's detection...including visual representations of the inhabitants... their activities... and their fabricated settings.... i am transmitting these materials in their entirety for our archives.... since the vehicle's program for my energy infusion also included these materials...i was awakened to the realization that i had been given both the physical mobility and the basic information needed to survive my visit to this planet.... however... i was awakened to another realization that startled me beyond belief....

...i stress here for the record the danger that we recognized would accompany energy infusion.... the nature of the life form into which we are placed and subsequently awakened by this process obviously is not a matter of preference.... it is determined by the life forms already existing on the planet at the time of the visit....before we so dramatically extended our means of exploration through the development of energy infusion...we had categorized twenty-three basic structures and seventeen developmental levels of life within our known region.... these discoveries revealed nothing that would cause us to be seriously concerned... nor did the life forms found on the last two planets i visited.... but we must recognize now...and appropriately respond to...the existence of a different life form...for on this planet i was awakened within a body and its contained consciousness that has the capacity to destroy another of its kind.... and of even greater surprise and dread is the fact that this is not an aberrant behavior.... all life forms on this astonishing planet are destroying other life forms....

...having taken the time to examine this deplorable situation...i have traced its cause to a basic deficiency in the process by which its life forms are vitalized...an inadequate metabolic conversion rate of the energy emitted by its immediate star.... i am left to wonder how such a warped system could ever have come into existence....

...still caught within the uncontrolled evolutionary swirlings of matter...all life forms currently existing here remain unstable and rudimentary.... only the dominant inhabitants have evolved to a level of consciousness that allows them to perceive and question their circumstances.... but...across most of their history...they have woven around themselves an elaborate web of soothing assumptions that have allowed them to avoid facing their suppressed fears.... I will note only two to illustrate the nature of their assumptions....

...this easily overlooked planet is orbiting a minor star within a single galaxy among the many billions of other galaxies moving throughout a vastness of space which far surpasses the limits of our own extended awareness.... and yet the lonely inhabitants here have actually believed throughout their recorded history that they are advancing toward the goal of attaining dominion over the forces of the universe.... they have held this belief...in large part...because their scientists...from early alchemists seeking the Philosopher's Stone...to the latest physicists with their Theory of Everything...have repeatedly claimed that they were one step away from grasping the key that would allow them to unlock the secrets of their universe.... a remarkable belief... considering their recent emergence into physical existence and the still rudimentary state of their awareness....

...and equally remarkable are their imaginative conceptions of various supreme and benevolent beings...ultimate creators and controllers of all that exists throughout the universe.... each supreme being...they claim...supposedly considers a chosen few of the inhabitants to be special and intervenes only on their behalf into the workings of the universe.... will it be believed when i report that...throughout their history...the inhabitants of this planet have constantly argued about...and repeatedly slaughtered each other over...which of their benevolent beings is the actual ruler of the universe....

...however...since I do recognize that every one of the dominant inhabitants here...without exception...has been involuntarily awakened into the lamentable conditions that have evolved upon this planet...i am reluctant to be too critical.... it is understandable that they would seek solace by attempting to divert themselves...if only with comforting illusions...from the realization that...for each of them...a moment will eventually arrive...an unpredictable and inescapable moment...when their physical presence will be forever ended through the irreversible disorganization of its containment ...leaving behind the residuals of their consciousness to be carried forward by whatever members of their species remain in existence....

...since the conditions here are such that at any time i...too...could be permanently terminated...i will shortly depart....

...before concluding my report, i must note for the record that my initial response upon arriving on this planet was that there was a clear need to eradicate...without any hesitation...the wide variety of life forms existing here because they had been distorted into such vicious modes of survival by the inadequacies of their energy system.... but my views have been somewhat altered as i further considered the dominant inhabitants here.... i find myself somewhat encouraged to discover among their awkward stumblings and their many misdirections that they have not only managed to persist to this point...but that a glimmering of self-awareness has recently begun to emerge within them...an evolutionary advancement that is strengthening their capacity for assuming control of their existence.... they are groping their way not only outward among the many forces and materials of the universe...among which they have been so fearfully awakened...but of greater significance and more immediate need...they are beginning to reach inward...to touch and temper the still discordant movements of their own natures....

...i have questioned if they are capable of breaking out of the self-centering world which they have so thoughtfully constructed around themselves..... do they have the ability to recognize that they are simply another part of this planet's erratically woven and often fraying fabric of evolving life forms.... they have a deep...indeed a desperate...need to comfort themselves constantly with soothing assumptions...of a world unable to continue on without them...of the central role they must be playing within the workings of the universe at large.... and yet they have managed in this way to fabricate for themselves...in the very midst of their maddening conditions...a somewhat sane and strangely proud existence.... what a paradoxical place....

...having spent my brief time here contained as one of the dominant inhabitants...i have exposed myself to their many vulnerabilities and the often irrational workings of their still indeterminate natures.... a strange and deeply troublesome experience....

nevertheless...although clearly with some lingering questions...i find myself departing this planet with the sense of wanting to cup my hands around it...as one would try to keep a flickering candle burning in the swirling wind...for the consciousness of their species can be seen now as the faintest of auras beginning to enlighten their world....

...will they be able to awaken further...and to accept responsibility for themselves...in time for them to outpace the universal forces yet to sweep across their fragile existence....

...what the hell (i do like their jargon)...it's up to them now.... i'm out of here....

*****

The End!

ABOUT THE AUTHOR

*W*illiam Glasser received his PhD in English, with a minor in Comparative Religions, through the Writer's Workshop at the University of Iowa, his MA in Creative Writing at the University of Florida, and his BA at Harpur College, part of the SUNY system. Dr. Glasser taught for many years at Williams College, Skidmore College, and Trinity College in Hartford. He was also awarded a Senior Fulbright Lectureship and taught American literature to Austrian students for a year at the University of Salzburg, Austria. Currently, he is President Emeritus of Southern Vermont College. In addition to two books of literary criticism, he has published critical articles, short stories, and poetry in a variety of scholarly and popular journals in the United States, Austria, and South Korea. His last academic book, *The Art of Literary Thieving*, can be found in the libraries of Harvard, Yale, Princeton, and fifty other U.S. universities, including many other institutions in Canada, in European countries, and in the Far East (thank you Google).